TAINTED LOVE

STACY CLAFLIN

TAINTED LOVE
AN ALEX MERCER THRILLER #6
by Stacy Claflin
http://www.stacyclaflin.com

Receive free books from the author sign up here: https://
stacyclaflin.com/newsletter/

GRAB

The woman's heart raced. Her mouth went dry. She took a deep breath and paced the park. Nerves always got the best of her at this point in the game.

But it wasn't a game. Not really.

Well, maybe.

She rubbed her rounded belly. It felt awful, like every other time. Itchy. Heavy. Awkward. Somewhat stiff. Not like the real thing would be.

The fake pregnant belly was the closest she would ever come to actually having a child grow inside her. But she would be the only one to know that.

She continued rubbing as she walked the perimeter of the playground. Looking. Waiting.

Still no security cameras—that was why she'd chosen this one. And because a lot of young moms frequented it. She'd done her due diligence. Trees blocked the view of the street. Nothing to get in the way. Moms with baby strollers came as early as the sun lit the sky to get out of the house, away from their husbands. Not that she blamed them.

The woman adjusted her floppy hat on the brown wig. The

fake hair was even itchier than the belly. She hated the whole getup, but it was part of the process.

How else would she get—and be able to keep—her next baby? Nature wouldn't help her out. The most advanced medical technology hadn't done squat.

And best of all, this way she didn't need a man to get what she wanted. Dealing with her exes had been the worst part of the ordeal, other than the heartbreak of not being able to pass on her DNA. She couldn't push a kid out between her legs and she couldn't adopt because of... Well, she didn't want to think about that.

None of that mattered anymore. The only thing that did was getting a baby, and this was her day. She could feel it. Something good was in the air.

Her heart sped up again at the thought.

If anyone would get to the park. She glanced around, not seeing a single soul.

Where were the new moms? The other mornings, they straggled in one at a time before things got busy after breakfast.

At this rate, there wouldn't be any stragglers. She'd have to wait for nap time when things thinned out.

She took a deep breath. It would be fine. One way or another, she'd return home with a baby to put in the empty crib. A baby to dress in the clothes already hanging in the closet.

It was all a matter of patience. She'd done this before and she'd do it again.

A crow flew down near her, cawing loudly.

She jumped and walked over near the trees. The sun was already getting warm. Between that and the fake belly and wig, she would overheat before too long.

Crunch, crunch!

A car in the parking lot.

Squeal! Crunch!

Brakes.

Her heart nearly jumped into her throat.

This was it! The first opportunity of the day. She pulled a mirror from her purse and practiced her sweetest smile. It was perfect. She looked innocent and trustworthy.

The chestnut wig even made her resemble an actress who was famous for being kind-hearted and generous. It gave others a sense of familiarity, made them feel like they already knew her. Like they could trust her.

A wicked smile slowly spread across her mouth, but she quickly covered it up.

Footsteps sounded.

Her pulse drummed in her ears, making it hard to hear anything else for a moment. She pressed a palm against a tree and pretended to stretch. So freaking awkward with the belly and the hair getting in the way.

No matter. It would all soon pay off.

Assuming the person walking her way had a baby.

Squeals and the patter of feet sounded.

The woman turned around. Relief washed through her.

A baby stroller and a mom with dark circles under her eyes. Two little kids ran ahead of her, heading straight for the toddler playground. She called to them to be careful.

A tired, distracted mom. Could this get any better?

The woman glanced back at the trees to the path she'd take to her car. She hadn't parked in the lot, so nobody would be able to describe her vehicle to the cops, but she was close enough that no one on the road would notice her racing away from the park.

She continued pretending to stretch before jogging delicately over to the bench where the mom sat, yawning.

"Long night?" She gave her rehearsed sweet smile.

The mom nodded and rubbed her eyes. "I always forget how much newborns wake up at night. Your first?" She glanced at the fake pregnant belly.

"Yeah. We're so excited."

"Congratulations."

She sat and held out her hand. "Thanks. I'm Jessica."

"Lauren."

They shook hands and made small talk while she peeked at the sleeping baby. Couldn't be more than a month old.

"How old?"

"He's nineteen days. No, twenty. Is it Wednesday?"

Jessica gave the mom her most sympathetic smile. "Thursday."

Lauren's eyes widened. "Really? The days really do run together. I better order groceries before the weekend."

"It'll be here before you know it."

Crying sounded near the slide. Lauren jumped up, keeping a hand on the stroller, and looked in that direction. "Are you okay, Brooklynn?"

The toddler wailed. "I bleeding!"

Lauren leaped over to the slide and knelt over the fussing girl.

Jessica looked back and forth between the baby and Lauren, who was now dealing with two crying tots.

It didn't get any better than this.

Jessica leaned over toward the infant while watching Lauren from the corner of her eye.

Still distracted.

Hands shaking, Jessica undid the buckles. They were the same as those on the car seat in her backseat. She scooped the baby into her arms. Shot a glance at Lauren, who still had her back to them.

"Stay quiet, Sammy," she whispered to the baby.

Then she ran.

NORMAL

Alex Mercer clocked out then headed for the captain's office. Through the blinds, he could see his best friend typing on his laptop.

Knock, knock!

Nick glanced over and waved Alex in.

Holding back a yawn, Alex pushed the door open and entered. "Morning."

"I have good news."

"Yeah?" Alex sat across from his friend.

"Chang is moving and—"

"That *is* good news." Alex rested his hands behind his neck and grinned. Captain Nick Fleshman and Officer Chang had been at odds for over a year.

Nick snickered. "I didn't mean it like that. His absence leaves room for another officer to work the day shift."

Alex arched a brow. "There are others with more seniority than me. I don't want to take advantage of our friendship."

"You're not." Nick glanced at his computer screen. "Nobody else is interested in days."

"Really?"

"It's true. What do you say? Interested?"

Alex thought about it. Night shift was working pretty well for him and Zoey, but days probably *would* be better.

"You'd be able to see Ariana more. Make it to more of her softball games."

He couldn't deny that would be a benefit. Alex stopped by the middle school ball field when he could, but it wasn't the same as being able to watch his daughter's full games.

"What do you say?" Nick arched a brow.

"When do I start?"

"I knew you'd say yes." Nick clacked away on the keyboard. "Two weeks."

"Perfect. Ari will be thrilled."

"So will Zoey." Nick glanced at him. "How are you two doing? The newlywed period is going well?"

"Newlywed? We're coming up on our first anniversary."

"The newlywed period is the first two years."

"Really? Well, it's as great as it can be with three kids. We're a little overwhelmed with the newborns."

"Newborns? Laney and Zander are three months old now."

"True." Alex yawned. "But they still wake up all the time. It's twice the work with two of them. Twice as exhausting. Zo and I barely have time to feed ourselves, much less time to plan anything for our anniversary."

"You'd better get home and let her get some sleep, then."

"And some sleep for myself." Alex rose and stretched, trying to hold back another yawn. "We still getting the kids together for a movie night?"

Nick nodded. "Let me double-check my schedule for the exact date. You two don't have to stay. Just drop off Ari."

"We want to hang out. It's been too long since we've hung out with you and Genevieve. Speaking of marriage…" Alex let his voice trail off.

Nick cleared his throat. "I picked out a ring."

"You did?"

"Yeah, now it's a matter of getting five minutes alone with her to pop the question."

"Good luck with that." Alex snickered. Between Nick and Genevieve, they had four kids. Nick had his three and Genevieve had just adopted Tinsley, who she'd been fostering. "Once you get married, can she work here again? Or is that still a conflict of interest or whatever?"

He shrugged. "Not sure entirely. One thing at a time. She's really happy there, so I'm not going to push it."

Alex reached for the doorknob. "If you need us to take the kids for an evening, just say the word. Preferably on one of my nights off."

"Will do. Thanks."

They said goodbye, then Alex headed for the parking lot to his new-to-him sedan. Actually, it wasn't even new to him anymore. He'd had it about a year already, but it was such a step up from the beater he'd driven for so long, he still thought of it as new.

He picked up a mint mocha on the way home, knowing he'd be up with the babies for a while to let Zoey sleep. Lately, the twins had been on opposite schedules, meaning that someone needed to be awake at all times.

It was exhausting, but totally worth it. He was married to the woman of his dreams and they were an actual family. An unusual family, but it was theirs, and he wouldn't have it any other way.

Alex parked on the curb between his parents' house and Zoey's parents' house, where they lived. His in-laws had converted their three-car garage into a living space for Zoey and him. It was the best situation since the Nakanos had adopted and raised Ariana, Zoey and Alex's oldest. She was born when Alex had been only fourteen and Zoey, sixteen. Since they all wanted a hand in raising her, it was the least intrusive way to make it work.

Once inside, Ariana nearly crashed into Alex. He steadied his coffee cup.

"Sorry, Dad!" The thirteen-year-old flashed him an apologetic smile. "I'm running late. About to miss my bus!"

"Want me to drive you?"

"Really?" Her eyes lit up as she slid on her jacket. "Mom and the babies are sleeping, so she won't even miss you."

Alex gave her a double-take. "They're all three sleeping?"

"Crazy, right?" She stuffed some textbooks into her schoolbag.

"Let's go."

"Wait." Ari froze. "You're not driving a cruiser today, are you? It's always so embarrassing when you drive in that."

He snickered. "I *want* all those boys to know your dad is to be feared."

She groaned. "*Dad.*"

Alex put his arm around her and kissed her forehead. "I'm just teasing. Kind of. But no, I'm not driving a cruiser today."

Ariana breathed a sigh of relief. "Okay, good. Let's go."

He finished his mocha and tossed the empty cup in the trash before opening the door.

"Bye, Mimi and Papi!" Ari called to her grandparents.

They both called back their goodbyes. Just as Alex and Ariana stepped onto the front porch, the bus drove away.

"So glad you're here."

He ruffled her hair, which earned him a sideways glance. "Sorry. But I'm sure Mimi or Papi would've taken you. Or Grandma and Grandpa." Alex nodded toward his parents' house next door.

"Or Mom, if nobody else would."

He remote-unlocked his car then they climbed in, talking about her latest science project. By the time they reached the middle school, there was a line of cars.

"You can just drop me off here," Ari said before Alex turned on the property. "It's fine."

"Don't want people seeing me dropping you off?"

8

"Love you, Dad." She gave him a quick kiss before jumping out and running across the parking lot.

"Love you too, kiddo." He waited until she was inside the building before heading back to the house, half-tempted to pick up another coffee. But if Zoey and the babies were both sleeping, he might be able to get some shut-eye.

Back in the house, he waved to Kenji and Valerie as he passed through the kitchen on his way to the converted garage. His and Zoey's home. Dark silence greeted him. Alex's whole body relaxed. He couldn't remember the last time he'd been able to go to sleep right after his shift.

He went into the bathroom to clean up and change. Zoey and both babies were sprawled across the bed, leaving him little room. He climbed in, careful not to wake anyone, and fell asleep as soon as his head hit the pillow.

Soft cries woke him. It felt like he'd only gotten an hour of sleep, maybe less. He wanted to ignore the sounds but couldn't do that to Zoey, so he felt around to see if the fussing baby was close. Sometimes they just wanted to be cuddled and would quickly fall back asleep. Nobody was in bed, at least not within his immediate reach.

He sat up and looked around, rubbing his eyes. Zoey sat in the plush glider chair, rocking one of the twins. The other one was in the swing, cooing.

"Sorry," Zoey said. "Didn't mean to wake you."

"And I didn't want you to have to get up with both of them. Let me help."

She shook her head. "Go back to sleep. You need it. I actually got six straight hours of sleep today."

"Six? How'd you manage that?"

"They both slept that long, and at the same time, no less."

"Miracles do happen."

She smiled. "Now it's your turn for some sleep. I'll take them out to see my parents once I'm done nursing."

He climbed out of bed and gave her a kiss. "Are you sure? I don't mind helping."

"I know. You really are the best."

"Stop."

"No, I mean it. Some of my friends tell me they don't get any help at night with their kids. You help every day after working all night, hardly getting any sleep. And you agreed to live in this garage at my parents' house. I know that wasn't easy—we could have our own place."

Alex panned his palms around. "This *is* home, and it was easy because then we can all be close to Ariana. She doesn't have to decide which set of parents she wants to stay with, and it also gives us the chance to save money while you stay home. There isn't any rush for you to go back to work. This is the perfect situation, actually."

Zoey gave him an adoring look. "I don't know how I got so lucky."

"I don't know how *I* got so lucky." He kissed her again before also kissing both babies. Then he climbed back into bed.

CLUE

A lex woke to a bright and quiet room. He stretched, unable to remember the last time he felt so rested. It was at least three months—just before they had two newborns to take care of. The babies had been born full-term and didn't have any issues that multiples sometimes had. They were lucky in that regard. He couldn't imagine what it'd have been like otherwise. Two healthy babies were hard enough to deal with.

He took a minute to wake up before getting out of bed and cleaning a little. There was hardly ever any time for that with the two babies. Once everything was organized, he showered, dressed, then stumbled out to the main part of the house.

Everything was quiet there, too. So much silence, he almost didn't know what to do with himself. His stomach rumbled, reminding him to eat. He found some leftovers in the fridge and warmed those, checking his phone as he waited. Typical emails and blog post comments—nothing that couldn't wait. He was about to check social media when the microwave beeped.

Alex sat at the kitchen table with his food and nearly choked when he saw a private message. He ran a blog featuring missing persons cases, and one of the first cases had been solved. The girl had actually been found alive after nearly two years. Before Alex had gone to the academy, he'd put a lot of effort into getting word out about the case. It hadn't been easy—the teen had been into drugs and because of that, people didn't seem to care about her case.

His heart soared reading the message from the girl's mom thanking him profusely for his help.

The door leading to the back yard opened. "You're awake."

Alex spun around to see Zoey with a fussing baby in her arms. He got up and took the bundle from her. "And I have great news."

"You do? What?"

He told her about the found teen, and Zoey wrapped her arms around him. "I remember that girl. You worked really hard to get the word out about her. Good job."

"I didn't do anything much."

"Sure you did." Zoey kissed his cheek. "If you want to come outside, we're all out there enjoying the weather."

"Even Ari?"

Zoey nodded. "She got back from school about an hour ago."

"No wonder I feel so rested. You didn't need to let me sleep that long."

"I got six hours, so you deserve as much. I'm going to change her." She reached for the baby.

Alex darted away. "I'll do it, then I'll join you guys outside."

"You sure?"

"Yeah. I feel so lazy. May as well do something useful."

She snickered. "Thanks."

He went back to their apartment and changed Laney, who cooed and grabbed at him the entire time. Alex laughed and somehow managed to get her changed despite her squirming. She took a fistful of his hair as they headed back for the kitchen. He gently pulled her away and held her lower so she couldn't reach.

Outside, Ari was sprawled on a blanket playing peekaboo with Zander. The baby squealed each time his older sister moved her hands to reveal her face. Alex took a moment to take it all in. This really was the life. While things weren't perfect, he couldn't ask for anything more—especially given everything they'd all been through. Ariana kidnapped two years earlier, him nearly losing Zoey to another guy, Zoey getting abducted. Heck, even Alex himself had managed to wind up prisoner to a madwoman determined to rid the earth of cops. In the last year, nobody they knew had been in any kind of peril. In fact, life throughout their small town had been pretty boring, and he hoped it stayed that way for a long time.

Kenji threw some patties on the grill. They had an impromptu barbecue, and Alex's parents came over through the gate between the two yards. With so many loved ones there, he barely had two minutes to hold either of the babies.

Zoey slipped her arm around his waist and leaned against him. "It's almost too good to be true, isn't it?"

"Don't say that." He grimaced, thinking of how it would be all too easy for things to go awry. "I don't think I could handle another trauma happening. We've been through more than most people five times our age."

"Most people five times our age are dead."

"Exactly." He checked the time, glad to see he still had hours before he had to think about heading to work. "Oh, I have good news."

Zoey arched a brow. "Really? Did you get a raise?"

"No, but I might get to be on day shift soon."

Her mouth dropped open. "For real?"

"Nick said Chang is leaving, and he's offering me the shift."

"That's great news! If we can get the twins to sleep through the night, then we can all sleep at the same time." She yawned.

"Speaking of sleep, why don't you go get some before I have to leave?"

"I got six straight hours, plus I napped when the babies had their late morning nap. I feel great."

"Are you sure?"

She nodded. "Plus, Ari said she wants your help for her science project. If the babies sleep, then so will I."

"And if they don't? At least not at the same time? Aren't you worried it was a fluke?"

"I think it's the beginning of sleeping through the night." Her eyes lit up with excitement. "I think they're at that age."

"I hope so. Just let me know if you change your mind."

Zoey kissed his cheek. "Thanks, but I still feel great after such a good sleep."

Everyone finished eating, then Ari dragged Alex upstairs to help with her science project. He didn't feel like he did much, but that was probably for the best. It was her project, after all.

Once he made it down to the garage-apartment, Zoey and both babies were asleep in the bed. He kissed each one gently, then sat at the table with his laptop. It was tempting to get a quick nap before heading to the station, but he would probably only end up groggy.

An email caught his attention, so he opened it and read the message.

DEAR ALEX,

You're the same guy who runs that blog for missing kids, right? This is going to sound strange, but please hear me out. I'm a mommy blogger, and if you don't know what that is, it's exactly what it sounds like. I blog about my kids and life as a mom. It's a thing, and there are a lot of us.

Anyway, I'm really worried about one blogger in particular. She's completely stopped posting about one of her kids. No pictures, no mentions, nothing. It's really weird. Like the little boy was never born at all, except I know he was because he's in all her old posts. I don't really know what to do. I'm not sure about going to the police because I don't even know where she's from. She's never mentioned her location. At least, not that I've been able to find. Everything about where she lives is pretty vague, which is common safe practice for mommy bloggers.

I really hope you'll look into this and mention it on your blog, or at least give me an idea of what I can do. People have asked about her five-year-old son in the comments, but she deletes them rather than answering them. And that's quite unusual for her. Something's wrong. I know it, but I have no proof. Please let me know what you think.

Josie Matthews

BELOW THE MESSAGE, she'd left a link to the suspicious blog. Alex read over the message again, and it did seem strange. Strange enough that he clicked the link to check it out.

A big colorful banner loaded at the top of the screen with the name of the blog— *Organic Mama Escapades*. On the sidebar was a cartoon caricature of the mommy blogger, depicting her as having long, curly, honey-brown hair and large hazel eyes. Below that were links to popular posts, blog awards, and other mommy blogs. She didn't appear to list her name anywhere—just Organic Mama.

So, mommy blogs were really a thing. Who knew?

He wanted to ask Zoey if she ever read them or was even aware of them, but that could wait. Instead, he read the top post, dated that day. It documented a trip to a park with her three kids —a boy just over a year, a girl about three, and a girl about seven. With that age spread, a five-year-old would fit comfortably into the mix, but there weren't any mentions. And there were over twenty photos in that post alone.

Alex skimmed through the ten posts on the first page and found more pictures of the same kids plus a few of the mom's pregnant belly. None of her face and no mention of a five-year-old boy. He clicked to the next page of posts, curious to see if the older boy would be mentioned.

There it was. Halfway down the page, on the fifth post. Two

weeks earlier. The mom and kids went to a different park, but she had plenty of pictures of a five-year-old named Connor. The other kids appeared fond of him, based on the photos. They made silly faces, hugged, and played together.

The following posts were more of the same—outings with four kids, two boys and two girls. The kids all happy and acting like they belonged together. But then when Alex looked up at the newer posts, Connor was just gone. And now that he looked closer, the kids seemed sadder. He hadn't noticed it at first, but now it was obvious. They were missing Connor.

Given the blogger's lengthy posts chronicling every detail of their lives, something was more than a little off. Alex couldn't let go of the feeling that something was wrong.

But where had the boy gone? And why was there no mention of him for so long?

LIFE

Nick tucked in the sheets and kissed Hanna. "Have sweet dreams."

"Don't let the bedbugs bite." She giggled and held onto her doll, which was an almost-exact replica of the nine-year-old.

Nick's heart warmed. How long would she stay sweet and innocent? His older two were like night and day compared to their baby sister. Everything that had happened to the family hit Ava and Parker so much harder than the youngest Fleshman.

He blew her a kiss before closing the door then heading down the hall. Framed photos of the kids from days long gone lined the walls. Decorations Corrine had put up, just like she'd decorated most of the rest of the house.

Oh, how things had changed. Now, they were not only divorced but his ex-wife and her lover were in jail for life. Nick had moved into the house after her arrest and finally had all the time he wanted with his kids.

But things were far from perfect. Ava and Parker both carried deep wounds from everything their mother had put them through —the divorce, moving them across the country away from their dad, committing a felony in which Ava ended up held captive by Dave, her almost-stepdad.

It was a good thing they were all in counseling. Nick hated to think of how much worse things would be if the kids had to deal with everything without outside help. Ava and Parker sure weren't talking to him about their feelings. Not that he was the most feelings-oriented guy around. An air of emotional detachment helped him as police captain. Or maybe being captain helped him to shove aside his feelings. He'd be a mess if he felt everything he saw from the job. His personal life was more than enough for him.

Either way, it wasn't helping the kids. But the therapist was.

Nick's phone vibrated in his back pocket. He pulled it out. A text from Genevieve.

Thinking of you. Several kissing and heart emojis followed the words.

His heart warmed again. He wandered into his room and held the diamond engagement ring before texting her back.

Thinking of you too... He added emojis, making sure to include more than she had.

She sent back even more, then he sent back more until he was laughing so hard his stomach ached.

Ava peeked in. "You're worse than a teenager, Dad." But the fourteen-year-old with salon-black hair and blood-red lips was smiling.

Nick sat up and patted the bed. "Come in."

She sighed like she was put out but sat next to him. "What did I do now?"

"Nothing. Can't a dad just spend a few minutes with his firstborn?"

"I guess." She glanced at the ring. "When are you going to pop the question?"

"Whenever I get two minutes alone with her."

Ava grabbed the ring and slid it onto her finger and held it to the light. "I told you I can watch the kids. Take her out to dinner. Hell, take her for a weekend getaway."

"Language."

She rolled her eyes. "Like you don't hear worse at work all the time. I probably hear worse at school than you do from the cops."

"We have rules around here."

"Fine, whatever. All I'm sayin' is, I'll watch the kids. Tinsley and Hanna listen to me. You won't have to worry about a thing."

"I don't want to put you out."

Ava threw him an exasperated look. "I'm not going to break, Dad. Life is crazy and my mom is crazier, but I'm *fine*. Life has made me tough. I'm not weak."

"I'd never accuse you of that." Nick smiled. "But are you really doing as well as you say?"

"Yeah. I have good friends, family, and the newest phone. What else could I ask for?"

Nick could think of several things but didn't mention any of them.

A dark expression crossed her face for a moment before disappearing.

"What was that?" He sat up and studied her.

"What?" Ava's tone was defensive.

"That look on your face."

"I don't have any look on my face."

"A moment ago you did."

Ava let out a long, drawn-out sigh. "Dad, really. You worry too much. I'm not a case from work."

"No, but you can't deny that expression. Are you worried about something?"

She picked at her black nail polish.

"Ava."

A beat of silence passed before she looked at him. "I've been thinking about Mason."

Nick's stomach tightened at the mention of Dave and

Corrine's son. His children's half-brother, and possibly Parker's full-brother. Mason was also half-brother to Zander, one of Zoey and Alex's twins.

Could their life be any more complicated?

"Have you heard from Mason?" Nick asked. "Seen him? Why are you thinking about him?"

Ava groaned. "This is why I wasn't going to say anything."

Nick took a deep breath and thought about all the advice their counselor had given him. "I'm not going to get upset, but it is my job to keep you safe. If there's anything I should know, I hope you'll tell me. I love you, Ava."

"I love you, too, Dad." She handed Genevieve's engagement ring back to him.

"And about Mason?"

"Well, nobody knows where he is, right?"

"Correct." Nick frowned. The kid had disappeared around the time Corrine and Dave had been arrested, and nobody had seen him. He'd been staying with Dave's parents before running away. Nick had made sure the force kept an eye out for him, knowing he might go after Ava. He'd assaulted her before, but he also hadn't known they were half-siblings—though he had known they were going to be step-siblings.

Either way, the kid was sick, which wasn't surprising given his genetics. Two mentally-unstable parents didn't give him much of a chance at a normal life.

Ava sat up straight. "Let me know when you want to propose to Genevieve, and I'll clear my schedule. If you want help planning your speech or whatever, let me know. I can help you say something really romantic."

"You don't think I can be romantic on my own? I've won her over with my charm so far."

She half-smiled and stood. "I'm just saying I can add a little something. If you want the help. I'm sure she'll say yes either way. 'Night, Dad."

Nick studied her, wanting to ask more about Mason, but kept silent. If she was really worried, she'd say something. "Goodnight, sweetie."

Ava spun around and left the room, humming. Maybe she really was okay.

He held up the engagement ring, and his heart thundered. Were they really ready for the next step?

TEXTS

Ava flopped onto her bed and sighed. It sucked having to lie to Dad, but what other choice did she have? It wasn't like she could tell him she was in contact with Mason. He'd freak. Like, legit freak out.

But at least she knew where Mason was. He was far away, and that was where he needed to be. The only reason she replied to his emails and texts was to keep her enemy close. Friends close and enemies closer, right?

She shoved down the thought of him making moves on her that one Halloween and focused on the fact that he was her brother. Well, half-brother.

Her phone played the tune indicating she had a text.

"Please be Braylon."

It was Mason.

She threw her head back, but read the message anyway.

Mason: Talked 2 mom & dad?

Ava: Dave's not my dad.

Mason: Did u?

Ava: No.

Mason: Not even mom?

Ava: No.
Mason: Not very talkative, ru?
Ava: Homework.
Mason: I need u2 talk to them.
Ava: Talk 2 them urself.
Mason: I can't show up at prison!
Ava: And I don't want 2 talk 2 them!
Mason: It's important.
Ava: I'm going 2 do my homework now. Bye.
Mason: I'm in Boise.

She froze. He was in Idaho? As in, one state away? Mason had been staying in Kansas before. Her hands shook so much she couldn't read the phone's screen.

Mason texted her again, but she dropped her cell. Was he planning on coming to Washington? To find her?

Ava's stomach lurched at the thought. It was one thing to text him while he was halfway across the country, but to actually have to see him again? To risk him putting his hands on her again? No. It was too much. He was getting too close.

Her phone played the tune again. Another text.

What was she supposed to say? Did she dare ask if he was coming her way? Maybe she never should've responded to him in the first place. Too late for that now.

Another text came in.

She stuffed the phone under her pillow. It wasn't the time to respond. She needed to calm down and figure out what to say first. Be able to say the right things and quickly.

Knock, knock!

Ava swore. "Who is it?"

"Me." Parker.

Her other brother. Her real brother. The good one. Annoying, but good.

"Hello?"

Ava grabbed her phone, silenced it, then shoved it under her pillow. "Come in."

He opened the door and marched in, closing it behind him. Pushing his bangs out of his eyes, he looked directly at her. "You hiding something?"

Her stomach twisted. "No. You?"

"What would I be hiding?" He plopped down on her computer chair and pulled a string from his torn black skinny jeans.

"You tell me."

"Why do you look guilty?"

"I don't look guilty."

"Right, and mom's not in prison."

Ava glared at Parker. "Shut up."

"About what? Mom or you?"

She took a deep breath. "What do you want?"

"Do you think Dad's acting weird?"

"No. Do you?"

He shrugged.

"Why do you think that? I just talked to him. He's fine." She debated bringing up the proposal, but decided to keep quiet. Dad would tell Parker when he was ready, if he hadn't already. "Maybe he's worried about you. I think he worries about us more now."

"Maybe you," Parker snapped.

"What's that supposed to mean?"

"You were the one missing. The one who was *violated*. He has more reason to worry about you."

"Dave didn't touch me," she said quickly. "Not like that."

"But Mason did when we were at that Halloween party and—"

"I don't want to talk about it. It wasn't a big deal. I got him to stop." Ava glared at him to drop the subject. "Why are you bringing this up now? The counselor said—"

"I can talk about what I want." Parker crossed his arms.

"It wasn't a big deal," Ava muttered.

"He's our half-brother."

"Nothing happened!"

They stared each other down before Parker spoke again. "You think Dad's gonna pop the question to Genevieve?"

Ava hesitated. "Probably."

Parker scowled. "He's so selfish!"

"No, he's not."

"Yes, he is! After everything we've been through, he's going to get married and throw in *another* sibling into the mix. Like our family isn't screwed up enough."

Ava crossed her arms. "Mom was going to marry Dave, and you didn't have a problem with it. She moved us across the country away from all our friends. Then she worked with that jerk when he kidnapped me. You and Hanna were next, you know. Thank God Dad stopped it."

"Dad wasn't on that case, remember?"

"Officially. But you know he was working on it at some level since I was missing."

"Whatever. You weren't even here to know."

"Look. If you're just in here to bug me, then go. I have homework."

He glanced around. "I don't see any."

"It's in my bag. Go."

"Fine." He left without another word, slamming the door behind him.

Ava rolled her eyes. He was handling everything worse than she was, even though she'd been through more. She didn't have time to think about that because she really did have homework to do, and if she didn't get started, she'd be up all night.

Once she got her books on the bed, she pulled her phone out from under the pillow.

Four more texts from Mason.

Her stomach knotted. Should she respond and tell him to leave her alone, or would it be better to ignore him and get the point across with her actions?

Another text came in from him.

Anger boiled in her gut. She opened the texting conversation, read his string of annoying messages, and replied.

Ava: I told you I'm doing homework. Leave me alone.

Mason: I'll decide when I'll leave you alone.

She stared at the message, her hands shaking.

Mason: Got that? I decide.

RESEARCHING

Alex yawned and wiped something yellow off his pants. It was sticky, and he cringed. He'd just returned to the station after a drug bust, and he wasn't sure he wanted to know what the sticky stuff was.

"You want to take your lunch?"

Alex looked up to see Detective Sanchez. She looked as tired as he felt. He rose and stretched. "I don't get why it's called lunch at this hour."

"What would you call a three o'clock meal? It's too early for breakfast."

"It sure isn't lunch." Alex slid the paperwork into a file. "I'll see you in a half-hour."

"Sounds good, Mercer."

He gathered his things and nodded as he walked away. Now that he was on break, his mind wandered back to the mommy blogger. Something was definitely awry there. Kids don't just disappear into thin air, and parents don't simply go on as if nothing happened.

Alex knew that firsthand. At his lowest point, he'd been an uninvolved parent—he'd given Ari up for adoption and let Zoey walk out of his life. He only saw his daughter twice a year most years before her abduction. And even with all his issues, it had ripped his world apart when she went missing. He did everything in his power to find her, including telling everyone he could about the kidnapping.

Even as uncommitted and self-absorbed as he'd been at the time, there was no way he could have gone on with his life as if nothing had changed.

That was why he couldn't let go of the mommy blogger. Why had she suddenly stopped posting about her son? It was highly suspicious that she'd deleted comments asking about him.

He mindlessly ate his warmed-up leftovers from the barbecue as he scrolled through the blog posts. They seemed to go back forever. He stopped where he was and found his way to the very beginning. Eight years earlier. It was a blog about the mom's pregnancy. Her first pregnancy. The oldest was seven, so that made sense.

Alex skimmed through the posts and jotted notes in his phone about everything that struck him as odd. Not one picture of the mom's face—how strange was that? Worried about *her* identity but posted dozens of pictures of her kids daily. She also never mentioned a father. No pictures or mentions that identified where she was located. She blacked out identifying information on the ultrasound images. There weren't any pictures at the hospital. Not even any pictures of the baby at first, and when she did start posting those, she didn't show the baby's face for months. Then all of a sudden, the blog posts were filled with pictures of the baby's face.

Why go from nothing to overboard all of a sudden? It just didn't add up.

"You ready?" Detective Sanchez's voice pulled Alex back to the station.

He looked up at her, then down to his half-eaten burger. "Has it been half an hour already?"

She nodded. "And we have a holdup at the convenience store on Jackson and Twelfth."

"Again?" Alex stuffed as much of the food into his mouth as he could and shoved his phone into his pocket.

"That side of town is getting bad, and I can't see it getting better anytime soon."

Alex swallowed. "Do we have backup?"

"That'd be us. Archer and Davies are already on their way."

He finished his food and followed Sanchez to a cruiser. By the time they reached the convenience store, the other officers had already apprehended the suspect. But they got word of a home invasion, so they headed toward the mobile home park a few blocks away.

"Never a dull moment anymore," Sanchez muttered.

"The town's really changed," Alex agreed.

"This part, anyway."

By the time they made it back to the station, they'd arrested the burglar and pulled over two speeding vehicles, one of which had illegal drugs spread out on the dashboard.

Nick was clocking in when Alex entered.

"Long night?" The captain poured himself some coffee.

Alex nodded. "Hard to believe this is the same quiet town I grew up in."

"Time has a way of changing things." Nick sipped his coffee. "And not always for the better. We see the worst of it."

"Isn't there anything else we can do? It feels like we just keep putting out campfires when there's a raging forest fire."

"We're doing all we can. And there always was crime, even if you didn't see it."

Alex shrugged. "I suppose. Hey, can I ask you something?"

"Go for it."

"In your office?"

"Sure." Nick led the way and closed the door behind them. "What's up?"

Alex sat across from him and told him about the mommy blogger and the missing kid.

"I'm not sure that sounds suspicious, Alex." Nick raked his fingers through his hair. "I know we've seen a lot of child abductions, but that doesn't mean every kid out there is in danger."

Of course it wouldn't be easy to convince the captain. Alex drew in a deep breath. "What mother suddenly stops talking about one of her kids? I mean, really. Want me to show you the posts? She writes thousands of words a day about her four kids. Then suddenly, nothing on Connor."

"There could be something behind the scenes she doesn't want to broadcast to the world."

"Like what?" Alex leaned forward.

"Custody issues, for example."

"With just one kid?"

"Maybe all the children have different fathers. I'm sure she wouldn't want that getting out, especially if she's such a big name in the mommy blogger space."

Alex drew in a deep breath. "I don't buy it. Not for a moment, and I can't believe you do, either."

"Maybe he was a foster child, and she thought she'd adopt him? If it fell through, she'd be crushed."

Alex wanted to pull his hair out. "If he was adopted, she wouldn't have ultrasound and pregnant belly pictures! Or photos of him right after she came home from the hospital. Does that sound like a foster kid to you? And besides, would she even be allowed to blog about a foster kid and show his picture a million times on her popular website?"

Nick's mouth twisted. "Okay. Say something's wrong. Is she local?"

"I don't know where she is. She never posts anything that gives away her location."

"We can't take it on as a case if she isn't here in town."

Alex frowned. "Even though there's a missing kid? We can't

even look into it and then pass along what we find once we figure out where she is?"

"You know how things work around here, Alex."

He leaned forward and tapped the desk. "So, there's nothing we can do?"

"I didn't say that. You have your blog, and you've built a big following of people who like to help find missing kids. Use that platform."

"We have more resources here. That's why I haven't done much with my blog."

"Not because you have two babies at home and a new career?"

Alex took a deep breath. "Yeah, obviously that plays into it. What if I find a connection to our jurisdiction? Then will you look at it?"

"Of course. Why don't you go home and get some sleep?"

"Okay." He got up and yawned. "Goodnight. Or morning, or whatever it is."

"Get some sleep, Alex."

He waved as he left then headed home. Zoey was asleep with the babies again. Maybe she was right about their schedules changing. Imagine if all four of them could sleep at the same time and also be awake at the same time.

Once he got out of the shower, one of the babies was crying. He gave Zoey a kiss and took Laney from her. "Go back to sleep. I'll take care of her."

"Are you sure?"

"Yeah." He bounced the baby and tucked the blankets around Zoey, then changed Laney while he warmed a bottle for her.

While he fed her, he scrolled through more posts on his phone. When the blogger became pregnant for the second time, it was much the same as the first time—belly pictures, but never anything with her face, and no pictures at doctor appointments like the other bloggers had. Once she had the baby, she posted plenty of images of the older daughter with her new brother, but no pictures of his face until he was nearly six months old.

Laney finished eating, so Alex burped her. Then, after a quick cuddle, he lay her down to sleep. Just before he climbed into bed, he noticed a new post on her blog. He stopped to glance at it then froze.

Pictures of the family at a park.

Alex recognized the playground.

DEFLECT

Jess gritted her teeth as she deleted yet another blog comment asking about Connor. She should've known that not posting about him would make people curious. Her blog *was* really popular, after all. She'd worked hard for that status. Not just the popularity, but also the income. Without the ads, sponsored posts, and other money flowing in from her blog, she couldn't stay home and support her kids.

And she wasn't going to let this take her down. What she needed was a good cover story. A really good reason for why she hadn't posted about Connor for a long time. It had to be something people would believe. Something that would garner sympathy and stop the accusatory comments and emails. Something that would—

"Mommy!"

"Mom!"

Daisy and Willow burst into the room, shoving each other.

"Girls!" Jess glared at them. "How many times have I told you not to bother me when I'm working?"

Daisy glared at her older sister. "She's being bossy."

"She won't listen to me!"

Jess took a deep breath. Why wouldn't these kids ever listen? "Daisy, when I'm working, Willow is in charge. Willow, don't be mean to your sister. She's only three. You're seven—a big girl. Act like it."

Both girls pouted.

"I'm serious. What happens if I can't get my work done?"

The responded in unison. "We won't have food and nice toys."

"Exactly. Now go out there and be kind to each other, both of you. Quietly."

Daisy stepped forward. "Can we watch that new superhero movie?"

"You said we could," Willow added.

"Shh!" Daisy put her arm out, not letting her older sister step forward.

Jess counted to ten silently. Letting them watch the movie would at least keep them quiet. It would be easy, but parenting wasn't about what's easy. "You really think I should let you watch it after you interrupted me while working?"

The girls glared at each other but didn't respond.

"Here's what we'll do." Jess glanced back and forth between her laptop and them, trying to think of something fast. "If you two finish your chores—quietly—then you can watch it. But every-thing has to be done without disturbing me. Got it?"

They both squealed and exchanged excited glances.

"Is your brother still sleeping?"

The girls nodded.

"When he wakes, make him a bottle. Don't let him see the movie. Have him watch a baby show on the iPad, facing away from the TV. Okay?"

"Yeah! Thanks!" Daisy hugged Jess, then Willow joined in.

Jess hugged them back, her irritation melting. "Thank you. Remember your chores first."

They scrambled out of the room, talking about the movie. Jess wasn't originally going to let them watch it because the genre was so violent, but if it would keep them busy for a while, it would be worth it. Besides, they'd been driving her crazy begging to see it.

She rubbed her neck and yawned. Sammy had been up a lot the night before. Of all the kids, he was the one who slept the worst. The others had all slept through the night long before turning a year old. Not this one.

But she'd survive. She always did. And besides, she may as well be used to a crappy sleep schedule. It would soon be time for another baby. She rubbed her well-used fake belly, which would need an upgrade to the next size up before long.

Crash!

Jess held her breath and counted. No crying, no yelling. Whatever the girls had knocked over probably wasn't a big deal. She waited a moment before turning to her computer screen.

After typing in her password, her blog's dashboard greeted her. She clicked over to the comments section and grinned when she saw how many new comments had come in overnight. But then her smile faded when she saw that more were asking about Connor than not.

She should have known it wouldn't be as simple as not mentioning him. She needed a story. Something believable, something that would garner sympathy. But not something that would bring too much attention. The last thing she needed was for her fans to feel sorry for her and start an online funding campaign or something of the sort. She needed a story that would fit with everything she'd ever revealed on the blog. And not only that, but a believable reason for not bringing it up before this.

It was a good thing she'd given the girls permission to watch the movie. Jess was going to need every minute to think about the perfect cover story—something she really should've put more thought into before—and then write about it in such a way that wouldn't make people suspicious.

But what could she tell them? It wasn't like she could say she'd shipped her five-year-old off to boarding school. She definitely couldn't say anything that would make it sound like he was hurt or sick. That would bring too much attention. What she needed was something that would make people feel bad but move on and stop asking questions.

That was all she needed, for the questions to stop. People would move on once they heard a story that would satisfy their curiosity.

Jess let her mind wander as she approved and responded to comments that had nothing to do with Connor. She thanked people for their compliments of the pictures. Answered questions. Then visited other blogs and left comments. The comment-swapping was a major part of getting more eyes on her blog. Part of the job.

By the time she was done, she leaned back in the chair and listened to the explosions from the movie. The girls shrieked, obviously enjoying themselves. And Jess would be the real hero, having finally let them watch one of those movies.

She smiled, enjoying the moment. Then the answer she'd been looking for struck her—the perfect story. Believable, sympathetic, and completely move-on worthy.

Now it was just a matter of crafting the perfect post and getting readers to believe why she'd waited so long to say anything.

Jess glanced at the time. About an hour before the movie ended.

Perfect. Absolutely perfect timing.

Assuming there were no interruptions.

DOUBTS

"You're still awake?"

Alex looked up from his laptop and gave Zoey a tired smile. "Yeah. Probably should get some sleep."

She rubbed his shoulders and gave him a quick kiss. "I'd think so. What's keeping you up?"

He turned the screen toward her. "This mommy blogger."

Zoey gave him a quizzical glance. "A mommy blogger is keeping you awake?"

Alex quickly explained everything he knew, then found the post with the pictures at the park from just outside of town. "We've been there. Remember?"

She leaned closer and scrolled up and down the post, examining the photos. "Maybe."

"Maybe?" Alex exclaimed. "It's that one park. I wish I could remember the name, but we met your cousins there when they were in town. I know we did."

Zoey pulled up a chair. "That was at least a year ago."

"Almost two. Not long after Ariana's whole ordeal."

"Her kidnapping."

Alex's stomach squeezed. The guilt of having been the one there when she was taken would never ease. "Yes."

"So, you think the woman lives in the area?"

"What other explanation is there?"

Zoey didn't look convinced. "Maybe she was visiting. Are there other places you recognize?"

He shook his head. "But she also doesn't post any kind of identifying information. That's not the point, though. Her kid is missing, and she isn't even talking about it! Who does that? She has a huge platform."

"Maybe he's not missing."

"Where is he, then?" Alex went back to the older posts. "Look. He's in so many pictures—for five years! Then suddenly, nothing. Not even a reference as to why he isn't in any of the photos. And why doesn't she ever post pictures of her face? Why doesn't she post pictures of the babies' faces until they're nearly a year old? And why—?"

"Slow down, Alex. There are probably good reasons for it all. She's protecting their privacy. Who knows? It could be common practice for mommy bloggers."

"It's not!" He clicked on another tab. "Look at this one. The mom posts all kinds of pictures of herself with the kids. At least a couple in each post. And look at this one." He switched to a different tab. "Same thing. And this one."

Alex showed her half a dozen other mommy blogs, and not one hid the mom's face or the baby's faces. All the other ones showed doctor visits, pictures of the blogger—everything the suspicious one didn't.

"You're making my head spin." Zoey rubbed her temples. "I need to get a shower before the babies wake. Can you get them if they wake before I get out?"

"Yeah, of course." He clicked back over to the blog in question.

Zoey kissed his cheek and rose. "Get some sleep, Alex. I'm sure there's a perfectly reasonable explanation for all of this."

He gritted his teeth. "Yeah. There's a missing kid, and the mom isn't concerned at all."

"I love that you care so much about the boy, but let her local police handle it."

"There's no way to know which precinct that is. She has her IP hidden and she doesn't post any identifying information. The only clue is that she's been to a park near here."

"She *may* have been to that park. Honestly, it could be any park, anywhere. Sleep on it, and see how you feel then. If you can't let it go, then post about it on your blog. You have the perfect platform for it. Your followers want to find missing kids as much as you do. But you're tired now, so don't make any decisions yet. Wait until you have a clear and refreshed mind."

Disappointment washed through him. "You really don't see anything wrong with all of this? If you blogged about our kids, would you suddenly stop posting about one of them?"

Zoey frowned. "No, but we also don't know what's going on. Looking at the pictures, I'd say she's a mom who cares about her kids. Why else would she take the time to upload so many photos and write about their daily events? There has to be a good explanation."

"Then why doesn't she just say what it is?"

"Sleep on it, Alex." Zoey yawned. "I smell like spit-up, and I need to get in the shower."

Alex yawned because of her yawn. "Fine, but you'll see. Something's wrong with this situation. Really wrong."

She squeezed his hand. "Will it make you feel better if I look at the blog while you sleep?"

"You'd do that?"

"Yes. Now get some sleep."

Alex climbed into bed and checked on the twins. Both Laney and Zander slept soundly. Their soft breathing made him realize just how exhausted he actually was. He fell asleep as soon as his face made contact with the pillow.

When he woke, he was alone in the bed. Laughter sounded from the main part of the house. It sounded like Ariana. Afternoon already?

He stretched and grabbed his phone, then checked the mommy blog. No new posts, and he was still convinced that one post was taken at the local park. It had to be. The playground was the exact setup, and he would swear even the trees in the background were the same. Maybe he'd take Ariana there to confirm his suspicions—if he could convince his thirteen-year-old to go to a park. They might have to take her little cousin. Macy and Luke's little guy loved swings and slides.

Alex sat up and called Nick.

"Hey, Alex. What's up?"

"If I could provide proof that blogger is from around here, can I look at the case with police resources?"

Nick sighed. "Have you gotten any sleep?"

"Yes, and this is a missing boy. Doesn't anyone care?"

"We don't know he's actually gone."

"Too many things don't add up. There's no other conclusion."

"Use your blog, Alex. If you come up with definitive proof that the boy is missing *and* that they live in the area, talk to me. As it is, I have five days' worth of paperwork to get through."

Alex drew in a deep breath. "Okay. Hey, if you want me to take your kids so you can have some alone time with Genevieve, just say the word."

"You going to take them to the park on the blog?"

Alex opened his mouth then closed it. His best friend knew him too well. "Just let me know if you want me to watch them. Ari would love the company."

"Will do." Nick's tone held a laugh to it. "Talk to you later."

"Bye." Alex ended the call and took a deep breath. Why was it so hard to convince Nick and Zoey the kid was missing? Something was wrong, and every minute that passed was a minute the child wasn't being helped—if it wasn't too late already.

Could they be right? Was he jumping to conclusions and bringing his own history into a totally different situation?

Alex read over the message he'd initially received about the mommy blogger. The sender clearly believed something was wrong, and according to her, the blogger had deleted comments asking about the boy. If that wasn't suspicious, what was?

He skimmed over the blog posts from the last few months. The blogger had posted tons of pictures of Connor then suddenly stopped. It was like he never existed, except the old blog posts proved otherwise.

No, Alex wasn't wrong about this. Zoey and Nick had their doubts, but Alex was certain about what he knew. The boy was missing, and the circumstances were too suspicious to let go.

He needed to do whatever he could to remedy the situation. That meant he needed to post about it on his blog. Alex would need screenshots—lots of them in case the blogger decided to change the old posts—and he needed his post to be bulletproof. So convincing that even his wife and best friend couldn't deny something was wrong after reading it.

And to do that, he first needed to contact the blogger.

INTERRUPTED

J ess took a swig of wine and closed her eyes, trying to block out the crying for just a moment. She shoved the bottle to the back of the fridge and closed the door.

The crying wouldn't stop. Her headache wouldn't stop.

Willow shrieked, followed by the sounds of retching.

Halfway through writing her explanatory blog post, Daisy had burst into her room in a panic. The baby had thrown up.

Jess's stomach turned just thinking about it. Sammy had puked so much that the orange chunky liquid sloshed around on the highchair tray and spilled onto the floor. It had taken every bit of self-control not to blow chunks herself as she cleaned it up.

It was obviously a virus, because now all three kids were vomiting. She'd already done two loads of laundry—sheets and clothes. The stuff was everywhere. Kids were crying. Spewing. Miserable. Sammy now had a fever, and the girls were sure to follow suit.

So much for getting her post up today. Maybe if the kids managed to get any sleep, she could finish it up. Otherwise, she'd have to make a quick post about being sick. At least those tended to get sympathy and clicks—and clicks meant ad revenue. Sympathy was good, too. She needed that, especially before posting about Connor. Maybe this stomach flu wasn't such a bad thing, after all. It could be exactly what Jess needed, gross as all the partially-digested food was.

Willow called for her.

She took a deep breath, closed the fridge door, and trudged into the living room where all the kids were resting. The girls had buckets and Sammy was in his pack and play wearing only a diaper. He was covered in puke again, but this time he was playing with it.

Jess gagged and turned to Willow. "Do you need something, sweetie?"

"I threw up again!" Tears welled in her eyes.

"Do you want more crackers?"

Willow shook her head. "I'm hot."

"I want crackers." Daisy sniffled.

Jess sat between them and wrapped her arms around both of them. "I'll get you whatever you need, but first let me empty these buckets."

By the time she'd gotten all the vomit cleaned up, Sammy puked all over his pack and play again.

"Crackers?" Daisy pleaded.

"Cold wash cloth." Willow wiped sweat from her forehead.

Jess raced into the kitchen and brought out crackers for Daisy before running a washcloth under icy water and giving it to Willow.

Then Sammy threw up again. At least she hadn't cleaned him up yet.

One thing was certain. She wasn't going to get any blog posts up today. Not unless it was a short one-liner about how evil the stomach flu was.

Three hours later, all the kids were asleep and none of them had puked in the last hour. With any luck, they would sleep through the night. Or at least long enough for her to get her post out and get a little shut-eye herself.

Probably just wishful thinking.

Jess turned off the cartoon and found a station playing soft music. Maybe that would help them rest better.

All she wanted to do was climb into bed and sleep, but she had to post something. A one-liner sounded perfect. It would hopefully be enough to keep everyone off her back until she could write her post about Connor.

Yawning, she sat at her desk and started a new post. She kept it short and sweet, explaining how sick everyone was and letting her readers know that she'd have a regular post up as soon as possible. And of course that post would include the explanation about Connor, but she wasn't going to mention that yet.

Next, she approved good comments and deleted the ones asking about Connor. There seemed to be more of those each day, so she really needed to publish the post about him as soon as possible. But that would have to wait until she got some sleep. Her eyelids kept trying to close.

Just as Jess was about to delete the last comment, she hesitated. Something about it stood out. And it wasn't just that the comment was as long as a blog post. It was written by a guy. Men almost never commented. They were never interested in mommy blogs. It was almost entirely a mom's space.

Her heart raced faster with each word she read. The sleepiness melted away.

Alexander pointed out every discrepancy. He'd gone through her blog with a fine-toothed comb and put everything together. The man even recognized one of the parks she'd taken the kids to, despite her efforts to hide any identifying details.

Her pulse drummed in her ears. The room seemed to shrink around her. There was no way she was going to approve the comment. He had to know that. And if he thought she was going to respond, he was crazy.

How did he know about her blog in the first place? It didn't matter. She needed to shut him up more than anyone else. Everyone else just had questions, some were more demanding than others, but there was something different about Alexander. It sounded like he wanted to *do* something.

Like he might suspect what was really going on. She rubbed her fake belly, the closest she would ever come to experiencing the real thing. It was impossible that he knew. Or was it? He'd even pointed out her lack of proof of doctor's appointments. She'd always posted belly shots and ultrasound images—she downloaded them from pregnancy boards and hid the identifying information—but somehow it hadn't been enough to throw Alexander off.

She deleted his comment. Then she saw something that made her blood run cold. He'd sent the same exact message to her email. He'd hunted down her email address.

This guy was dangerous. Too close to figuring out the truth.

She needed to do something about him, and fast.

LATE

Ava tried to pay attention to the movie, but she couldn't stop thinking about Mason's texts. She was tempted to block him—the moron couldn't take a clue—but she needed to know if he was coming to Washington or staying in Idaho. Hopefully, he'd stay away but that seemed unlikely. Why else would he have traveled from Kansas to Idaho?

He was technically a runaway since he was supposed to be living with his grandparents—Dave's parents. But he'd taken off, supposedly with a girlfriend, but Ava was sure that was a lie. She couldn't picture anyone putting up with Mason. He might be able to hide his creepiness factor for a date or two, but not long enough to land a girlfriend.

"You watching this?" Braylon put his arm around Ava.

She looked around and realized everyone in the theater was laughing, except her. "I, uh, got lost in my thoughts for a moment."

He frowned. "You've been doing that a lot lately. What's going on?"

She shrugged. "I don't really want to talk about it here." Or anywhere.

Braylon nodded, his brows knitting together. "Okay. We can grab something to eat after."

Ava forced a smile. "Great."

It wasn't that she didn't want to eat with him. She adored Braylon. They'd been neighbors since moving into the house, and she'd fallen in love with him the moment she saw him—as lame as that sounded. She'd always scoffed at the idea of love at first sight, at least until she'd laid eyes on him. His intense blue eyes and the dark wavy hair falling over them had taken her breath away the moment their gazes locked, and she still had the same reaction after all this time.

She leaned against him and tried to focus on the movie's plot. Luckily, it was mostly explosions and car chases, so she hadn't missed much.

By the time the movie ended, she'd almost forgotten about Mason and his texts. Almost. In the ladies' room, she peeked at her phone. Twelve new texts.

"Anyone else would get a clue." She stuffed it back into her purse.

"Problems with Braylon?" Emma, a girl from school, gave her a sympathetic smile as she washed her hands.

Ava shook her head. "Family drama."

"Ugh." Emma grimaced. "For what it's worth, I'm glad it's not Braylon. You two are so cute together."

"Thanks." Ava looked to the side, feeling her cheeks warm. She'd never been a girly-girl but Braylon seemed to be slowly changing that.

"Well, see you later." Emma waved on her way to the door.

Ava returned the gesture and murmured, "Bye." Then she checked her makeup before heading out.

Braylon was talking to Emma and her boyfriend by the video games. He put his arm around her. "Aiden and Emma are going to play laser tag. I know we talked about getting some food. What do you think about laser tag first?"

Laser tag would mean she didn't have to talk about what was on her mind during the movie—Mason. Ava smiled widely. "That sounds like fun! I'm gonna kick your butt, though."

He chuckled, his eyes shining. "I'd like to see you try."

"Sounds like you're in." Aiden grinned. "My uncle owns the place, so if there's a long line, I can get us in without waiting."

"Even better." Ava leaned against Braylon.

The two couples headed to the parking lot, where the car Aiden had called for was waiting. At the laser tag park, they found teens and young adults lined up around the building.

"You weren't kidding about the wait." Braylon nudged Aiden.

Ava shook her head. "No, he wasn't. Remind me not to come here again on a Friday night without them."

The car let them off near the entrance. They made their way inside after Aiden spoke with the girl at the ticket counter.

"What do I owe you?" Braylon asked, pulling out his wallet.

"Nothing. She just let us in."

"What about the ride?"

"We were going to take it anyway. Don't worry about it."

"Seriously?" Ava asked.

Braylon laughed. "I think we just found ourselves new best friends."

"Don't thank me yet." Aiden looked around. "We still have to wait in line for the room. Which one do we want? There's a forest, a desert, an open field, and caves."

They settled on the caves and got in line. Once inside, Ava had more fun than she'd had in a long time. She couldn't remember the last time she'd laughed so much, and as promised, she kicked Braylon's butt.

Growing up with a brother, she'd played with more toy guns than she cared to think about and as a result, had great aim.

After a few rounds, Aiden had to take Emma home. As they headed to the parking lot, Ava checked the time and realized it was past her curfew. And she had three missed calls from her dad.

She swore as they approached the car—Braylon insisted on paying for that one.

"What's the matter?" he asked.

"It's after ten. My dad's pissed."

"Uh-oh. Want me to talk to him?"

"No, he'll probably kill you. Police captain's daughter, remember?"

"Busted!" Aiden gave Braylon a playful shove.

"He likes me."

"Not after this." Emma giggled.

Once they were seated, Ava texted him apologetically explaining that they'd lost track of time.

Dad: You're with Braylon?

Ava: And 2 others.

Dad: On your way home?

Ava: Yeah. I swear. Lost track of time.

Dad: We'll talk when you get here.

She groaned.

Ava: OK.

Braylon wrapped his arm around her. "I'll talk to him. Don't worry about it."

"I'm more worried about you."

He glanced at the texting conversation. "See how he asked if I was with you? Because he trusts me."

"Or because he wants to lay down the law." Aiden snickered.

Everyone teased Braylon until the driver dropped them off in front of Ava's house. They waved, then she turned to him. "I'll see you tomorrow."

"You think I'm going to let you face him alone? I'll have a man-to-man with him if necessary."

She winced at the thought.

"Come on."

"Really, just go home. It's fine."

"Nope." He put his arm around her waist and led her to the front door.

It opened before they reached the welcome mat. Dad appeared and blocked the door. "Almost ten-thirty."

"Dad, it was an accident. I had my phone on silent and missed my alarm reminder."

He crossed his arms. "Why did you do that?"

She hesitated. If she told him about Mason, he would forget all about the broken curfew. But then she'd have a whole other set of problems.

Braylon spoke. "They always say to silence cell phones at the movies, sir. She was just being a responsible citizen."

Ava held back a smile. *Sir.* Nice touch.

"How long was the movie?"

They explained the whole thing about running into Aiden and Emma and getting into laser tag for free.

"It won't happen again," Braylon insisted. "I promise. I'll make sure to set a reminder on my phone from now on, too, as backup. I'm really sorry."

She held her breath, knowing her dad wouldn't budge. He was going to ground Ava, and she and Braylon wouldn't be able to go anywhere together for a while. It was all Mason's fault. If he hadn't been texting her like a jealous boyfriend, she'd have never put her phone on silent. Maybe she *should* block him. Or maybe she should just pay closer attention to the time.

Dad looked deep in thought. He crossed his arms and then uncrossed them. Time seemed to stand still.

Braylon and Ava exchanged a worried glance. Her stomach knotted. This was going to be bad.

Dad cleared his throat. "I can't say that I've never lost track of time. It's happened to everyone. Just don't let it happen again. Okay?"

Ava's mouth fell open. He was going to let it slide?

"Yes, sir." Braylon stood taller.

"Daddy!" Hanna called from down the hall.

"I'd better see what she needs. You two say goodnight." He nodded toward Braylon, then marched down the hall and into Hanna's room.

Ava pinched herself. "I'm awake. Did he really just let us off the hook?"

A slow smile spread across Braylon's adorable face. "I told you he likes me."

"He's never done that."

Braylon cupped her face and gave her a quick kiss. "Goodnight. I'll text you in a little bit."

"Okay." She was still in shock that her dad hadn't laid down the law.

"Love you."

Ava turned and stared into his eyes. "Love you, too."

Braylon showed himself out.

She locked the door then headed for her room, where she took her phone off silent. Halfway down the hall, it buzzed with a text. She grinned. "That was fast."

But the text wasn't from Braylon. It was from Mason.

DECISION

Nick rolled the engagement ring between his fingers and took a deep breath. He knew he wanted to marry Genevieve. He also knew she wanted it. The kids all seemed to be on board, too.

Why was he so nervous? Genevieve was beautiful, smart, kind, and strong. She'd adopted Tinsley, a girl with more problems than a math book, and she also loved Nick's kids just as much. But Genevieve was still young—not even thirty yet. Nick was more than twelve years her senior and brought with him more baggage than an airport. He had three kids and a murderous ex-wife, but at least Corrine was in prison without a chance at bail.

Guilt pinched Nick's gut. *That* was why he hesitated in giving her the ring. Genevieve deserved better than he could give her. He could give her his heart, but was it enough? Was he being selfish?

The topic hadn't come up, but surely she would want a baby. And why wouldn't she? She deserved to have as many as she wanted, but if she jumped into Nick's ready-made family, they would have four kids between them already.

He would give her a baby. Heck, he would give her the world if he could. Tinsley, too. He adored them both and wanted them to have the very best—but was that really him?

Sure, it was what they wanted. Now. But would they wake up one day with regrets? Would Genevieve look at him on his fiftieth birthday and wonder what she'd been thinking, marrying someone so much older? Would Ava give her so much attitude that she would think he wasn't worth the trouble?

His door burst open, and Hanna ran inside. "Can I make breakfast, Daddy?"

Nick lowered the ring and sat up. "Sure. Just let me help you."

"Okay." She beamed and bounced onto the bed. "Is that the ring you're gonna give Genevieve?"

His pulse raced. "Yeah. What do you think of that?"

"I can't wait!" Hanna grinned. "Tinsley's one of my best friends, and she's going to become my sister. How cool is that? She always wanted a big family. Did you know that?"

Nick shook his head. "Did she tell you that?"

"Yep. We tell each other everything."

He smiled, relief washing through him. Maybe he was over-thinking his doubts. "Does she want to be part of our family?"

Hanna scooted closer. "She wants you to be her daddy, too."

Nick's heart jumped into his throat. "She does?"

"Uh-huh. And I want Genevieve to be my new mom."

His stomach knotted. "But your mom is alive."

She frowned. "I know, and she'll always be my mom. But she's in jail, and that's the only place I can see her ever again. It's not the same thing. Genevieve can be here and do all the mom things, you know?"

Nick ruffled her hair. "I get it. And she'll be happy to do all the mom things, but she also doesn't want to replace your mom."

"I know." Hanna jumped from the bed. "Hurry up. I wanna make breakfast." She skipped out of the room.

He looked at the ring again. Maybe it was time to make a date for the proposal.

"Daddy!" Hanna called.

"Hold on!" He climbed out of bed and tucked the ring into his nightstand before going out to the kitchen.

He and Hanna made bacon, eggs, and pancakes until the aromas finally drew out the late sleepers. Both Ava and Parker came out, rubbing their eyes and asking for coffee.

"It's going to stunt your growth," Nick said as he handed a mug to his son.

"Getting up this early is going to stunt my growth." Parker poured enough creamer to turn the black drink white.

Ava drank it straight. "Ahh, much better."

"Time to eat!" Hanna handed Ava a heaping plate, then gave one to Parker.

"Dang." Ava looked at her sister. "You must think I'm a football player."

Hanna giggled.

They all sat around the table and joked around. Nick's heart warmed, glad everyone was in good spirits. It was hit and miss with the older two, and even more rare that they were both happy at the same time.

Parker was the first to rise. "I'm going to Noah's. We're going to play flag football at the park with some other kids."

Nick arched a brow. "Flag football isn't code for something else, is it?"

"No, Dad." Parker threw his head back. "It's only flag football. Just because you see druggie kids at work all day doesn't mean that's what I'm up to."

"You're right. Sorry, kiddo. And for the record, I don't see druggie kids at work *all* day."

Ava snickered.

"Great. See ya." Parker spun around.

"Wait," Nick said.

"What?" Parker sighed dramatically and turned back around.

"Sit down. I just have a quick question for you kids."

Parker sat, then all three stared at him expectantly.

Nick cleared his throat. "I've spoken with all of you about this already in one manner or another, but I want to double-check. I want to ask Genevieve to marry me, but I also want to make sure you're all on board. That you want this, too."

Ava leaned forward. "We just want you happy, Dad."

The other two nodded in agreement.

"But we'll be adding two more people into the mix. Someone will probably have to share a room."

"I claim Tinsley!" Hanna raised her hand. "Please!"

Nick laughed. "I also have another question."

Parker groaned. "We know it'll change things, and we don't care. Genevieve's great. Tinsley's great. Can we go now?"

"Now you're changing your tone?" Ava gave him a double-take.

He crossed his arms. "None of your business."

"But you—"

"Enough!" Nick glared at them. "That wasn't my question, Parker. I was thinking that we, as a family, could ask the two of them. What do you think?"

Ava rested her chin on her palms. "It's sweet, but it isn't *romantic*. Ask her yourself. Blow it out of the water, Dad."

Nick gave her a double-take. He hadn't been expecting that response. "What do you mean?"

"I mean that you should do something really cool. So romantic that she can't say no. She—"

"You think she'll say no?"

Ava rolled her eyes. "You know what I mean. She'd say yes if you asked her in a shack covered in mud, but make it special. Make it about *her*. Not any of us kids. We appreciate you wanting to bring us in, though. Right, guys?"

Hanna and Parker both nodded.

Nick studied his oldest daughter, surprised at her insight on the topic. "I suppose you're right."

55

"Of course I am."

He held back a smile. "Okay. It's settled, then. Now I just need to figure out what to do. Have any ideas?"

"The playground!" Hanna grinned.

"Take her to a beach," Parker said. "Chicks love the water."

"Women aren't *chicks*, son."

He shrugged.

Nick turned to Ava. "You're full of wisdom today. What do you think?"

"Pinterest. That's where I get all my good ideas."

"I'll have to check that out." Nick rose. "Let's get these dishes cleaned up, then you can hang out with your friends."

The kids grumbled but helped. As they were clearing the table, Ava kept glancing at her phone.

"Braylon?" Nick asked.

"What?" Ava looked up with wide eyes.

"Is he texting you?"

"Oh, right. Yeah." Her tone was distracted. Off.

"Everything okay in paradise?"

She nodded. "It's great. He's grateful you didn't get mad last night. We both are."

Nick couldn't help feeling like she was hiding something. "You know you can talk to me about anything, right? And if you don't feel comfortable, you can talk to Genevieve about anything, too."

Ava turned to the dishes in the sink. "Thanks, Dad."

He watched her out of the corner of his eye. Over the next five minutes, she checked her phone three times. Each time, her expression darkened with what looked like worry.

And that made Nick concerned. If he couldn't get to the bottom of it, he'd have to see if Genevieve could.

His daughter was definitely hiding something.

OBSESSED

Alex bounced Zander as Ariana explained the last stage of her science project. Zander fussed and squirmed, making it hard for Alex to concentrate.

"Do you think that'll work?" Ari asked.

Alex stepped closer and studied her. "Can you say that last part again?"

"Maybe I should just wait until Zander falls asleep."

"I can listen." Alex lowered his son and rocked him. "Just repeat the last part."

Ari looked a little frustrated, but complied.

"That sounds great," Alex said when she was done.

"Really? You're not just saying that?"

"No. I mean it. You're definitely smarter at science than I am."

Her forehead wrinkled. "I know you're just saying *that*."

"Nope. Is Mr. Forbes still at school? You can ask him. I drove him crazy when I was your age. Actually, I think I had that effect on all of my teachers."

The corners of Ari's mouth twitched. "You couldn't have been that bad."

"Ask any teachers who were there thirteen years ago. I know there are a few of them."

"The dinosaurs," she teased.

"Easy there." Alex chuckled.

"I can't believe I'm almost half your age. Can you?"

Alex closed his eyes for a moment. "That's not something you need to worry about. Your mom and I—"

"I know, I know. I'm not going to follow in your footsteps. I'll be at least seventeen before I have a baby."

Alex's mouth dropped open. "That's not what I meant! Not even close."

She laughed. "Dad, I'm totally kidding. My plan is grad school before I even think about a family."

He breathed a sigh of relief. "You don't know how glad that makes me."

"I think I do." She looked at Zander. "He's asleep."

"Finally. I'll be right back."

"Don't worry about it." Ari sat at her desk. "I just wanted your opinion on the project. I can put it together myself."

"You sure?"

She opened her laptop and nodded. "Yep. I'll let you know if I need more help."

"Okay. I'll be right up if you do."

"Thanks, Dad." Ari smiled at him before turning back to her computer.

Alex's heart warmed. He wasn't sure how he'd ended up so lucky. Especially after being absent so many years. What he deserved was a snarky teen, one who gave him as much trouble as he'd given his poor parents.

He rocked Zander as he made his way down the stairs and into their apartment.

Zoey was hunched over Laney's crib. She turned when the door closed behind him. "Both asleep at the same time again?"

"Must be a twin thing." Alex snuggled Zander into his crib

before pulling Zoey into his arms and giving her a kiss. "How did I end up so lucky?"

She kissed him back. "I feel like the lucky one."

"Seriously?"

"Are you kidding? I could be married to Kellen right now. If you hadn't stepped back into my life at just the right time…" She shuddered.

So did Alex. "I thought we weren't going to use his name."

She laughed. "He's actually not that bad. He just isn't you. Actually, I heard he got engaged. Apparently, Mom's still friends with him on FaceChat."

"People still use that site?" Alex snickered.

"I think just Mom and Kellen." Zoey grinned. "I'm going to warm up some leftovers after I get dressed. Want to join me?"

Alex's stomach rumbled. "I think that answers that. I'll warm the food while you change."

"Thanks." She gave him a kiss then headed for the closet.

In the kitchen, he found a dish of lasagna then warmed a large helping in the microwave. While he waited, he checked his email. Still nothing from the blogger, though the read-receipt showed she'd opened it twice.

After putting the second plate in the microwave, he scrolled slowly through his inbox to see if she'd sent a separate message that he'd missed. She hadn't.

"What's so interesting?" Zoey asked.

Alex jumped and turned toward her. "I didn't hear you come in."

She chuckled. "Apparently not."

He slid his phone into his pocket and handed her a plate. They sat and dug in.

"So, what was so interesting?" Zoey repeated.

"I sent a message to that mommy blogger asking for an explanation. She hasn't replied."

STACY CLAFLIN

Zoey's expression softened. "You're really worried about that little boy, aren't you?"

He released a slow breath and nodded. "Something's wrong. It doesn't add up. I just wish I could prove she's local, then I could put police resources into this."

She put her hand on his. "Is there anything I can do?"

"You could look through the pictures on her blog and see if you recognize any of the places. If she is in the area, she has to have pictures of other places nearby."

"If you think it'd help."

"It'd be something. I need to get to the bottom of this."

She got some milk from the fridge and poured a couple glasses. "Have you posted on your blog about her?"

"Not yet, but I probably will. I don't want to spook her, you know?"

"Why not? Get the word out there. Your followers will probably feel the same way as you. Then you'll have a whole army of people looking into it."

Alex thought about it. "That's a good point, but if she knows people are looking into it, she could start taking down her posts— evidence. Or she could alter them, or—"

"But the Wayback Machine doesn't lie. She can change her blog, but her posts are indexed there. It may not catch every single thing, but more than enough."

"You're right. Why didn't I think about that?"

"Because two heads are better than one." She squeezed his fingers.

He kissed her hand. "You're so smart. Plus, I do have screenshots."

"See? Everything's going to be fine." She gave him a playful smirk. "Tell you what—after we eat, I'll go through her blog with a fine-toothed comb and you write your post. By the time we're done with her, she'll be forced to tell the truth."

They quickly finished the food, then returned to the apartment, careful not to wake the babies. Two hours flew by before Alex knew it. Laney woke, followed by Zander.

Alex picked up Laney and changed her diaper. He glanced over at Zoey, who was feeding Zander. "Did you see anything in the blog?"

"I think you're definitely right. It's beyond strange that she just stopped posting about Connor. If I had a blog like that, I could never stop posting about one of my kids. I don't get it."

"See? Something is definitely going on. Did you notice anything local?"

Zoey shook her head. "The woman is good at hiding identifying information."

"Because she has something to hide." Alex picked up Laney and snuggled her. "She's been hiding something since the beginning. It's the only explanation."

"It really is. How's your blog post coming? Did you post it?"

"I've got it all written out, but I need to proofread it before I publish it."

She switched Zander to the other side. "I can look it over if you want."

"That'd be great. You're much better at grammar and stuff than me."

"Did you see her latest post?"

"Which one is that?" Alex asked.

"It was posted last night."

"Last night?"

"Yeah. Super short entry. She said all her kids have a violent stomach virus, so she has no idea when she'll post next."

Alex frowned. "That's convenient. Especially since she posted it after I sent my email."

Zoey nodded.

They spent the next hour with the babies before taking them upstairs to Valerie and Kenji, who were delighted to watch their grandbabies. Alex checked on Ari, who didn't want any help with her project, then Zoey read over Alex's post.

She handed his laptop back to him. "I just made a few minor tweaks. It's really good."

He looked it over and liked the word choices Zoey had made. His pulse drummed in his ears as he held the cursor over the publish button.

She squeezed his shoulder. "Press it."

Alex held his breath for a moment. Then he published the post.

POST

Jess wiped vomit from her face and washed her hands. She'd lost track of how many hours straight the kids had been throwing up. One would ease up, then another would start in again.

She kept checking online medical advice, most of which said she should have taken them in to see a doctor. But that was impossible since the kids didn't have insurance. She would have to keep handling it on her own and hope for the best.

Good thing she didn't have another baby yet. She couldn't imagine dealing with the constant feedings and irregular sleep schedule while cleaning up puke nonstop.

But even with all the distraction, she couldn't stop thinking about Alexander. He was too close to the truth. Closer even than anyone else who had commented asking about Connor. He'd really done his research. And he'd emailed her, too.

He wasn't going to be thrown off the trail very easily. At least she could prevent any of his comments from ever being published on her blog. Every single comment had to be approved by her these days.

What if he did more than just try to contact her? He could go to the authorities or the news. If he had any kind of platform himself—like if he had a video channel or a lot of followers on social media, he could bring a lot of unwanted attention to her.

That was why she'd been so careful to keep her posts free of identifying information. It would be impossible to tell where she lived. Where she spent time. She didn't have friends, so nobody would be able to point her out. They weren't regulars anywhere, so random waitresses or bank tellers couldn't identify them. Nobody was likely to recognize the kids.

She'd taken all those precautions precisely for a time like this. They would be okay. She would need to up her game, that's all. Get more creative. No big deal.

If only her kids would stop throwing up.

"Mom!"

"Hold on!"

Barfing sounded from the next room.

Jess's stomach lurched, but she closed her eyes and took a deep breath. She was more than determined not to let the messes get the best of her. And she certainly wasn't going to get sick.

She ran around between the three kids and the bathroom until by some miracle they all fell asleep in clean clothes.

Jess collapsed on the plush rocking chair and wiped sweat from her forehead. As tempting as it was to close her eyes and sleep, she needed to check her blog and publish the post she started that explained why she hadn't mentioned Connor. She clicked over to her website.

A choice she regretted immediately.

There were over a thousand new comments awaiting moderation. A thousand! On a normal day, she had maybe fifty. And that was when she posted about something fun she and the kids did. Lots of pictures and narrative.

Not after posting a quick one-liner about the kids retching all over the place.

Her pulse drummed as she clicked over to look at the new comments.

They were worse than she thought. Each comment demanded to know what happened to Connor. Some threatened to hunt her down. Others called her a murderer. And it actually got worse from there.

Jess didn't recognize any of the names. These were all people new to her blog. How did they find her?

She clicked away to the blog post and skimmed it over, making a few minor changes before pressing publish. There had been more she'd wanted to add, but there wasn't time for that. This situation needed to be brought under control right away.

Once the post published, a small amount of relief washed through her. Just enough for her eyelids to grow heavy.

The new post would have to do for now. It answered a lot of the questions. Hopefully well enough to get everyone off her back and focus on someone else. Exhaustion pressed every inch of her body, demanding sleep. And since she had no idea how long it would be until one of the kids woke to start yakking again, she needed to get what rest she could manage.

After checking on the kids, Jess climbed into bed and fell asleep as soon as her head hit the pillow.

When she woke, she felt rested and the house was quiet.

She bolted upright. With sick kids, she shouldn't be rested nor should everything be so quiet. Her breath hitched. She glanced at the clock. Eight hours. She'd gotten eight hours of sleep.

Was it possible the kids had slept that long? That the barfing part of the virus had passed? Or was it more likely that something was wrong? Could someone have figured out where they lived and taken the kids from her?

Jess slapped herself. It wasn't the time for ridiculous thoughts. Of course nobody had found them. She'd not only hidden their location and identities, but she'd done plenty of things to throw people off track. To make them think things that weren't true.

She jumped out of bed and raced into the living room.

All three kids were snuggled together on the couch watching a cartoon. Sammy was sucking on a bottle and the girls both had Popsicles.

Jess looked at Willow. "Did you get those?"

She nodded. "I thought it'd be okay."

"Yeah. Of course." Jess leaned against the wall and took a deep breath. "You're all feeling okay?"

"Hungry." Daisy frowned.

"I told her we had to take it easy," Willow said. "Our tummies aren't ready, right?"

"Exactly. I can make some soup or get you some crackers."

"Soup," Daisy said.

"Crackers," Willow insisted.

"We can do both. Just sit tight." Jess went to the kitchen and emptied the canned soup into a pot. While it heated, she checked her blog stats on her phone. While the views had exploded, the comments had, too. Now there were over two thousand in the queue.

Jess closed her eyes and took a deep breath. This wasn't something she could just ignore. Especially since most of the comments on her newest post expressed disbelief in her story about Connor.

However, luckily for her, a number of her regular commenters believed her. Sympathized with her, even. She approved those comments. Let the haters read those and see how wrong they were for ganging up on a single mom doing the best she could.

"Mom! I'm hungry!"

Jess set her phone on the counter, turned to the steaming pot of soup, and yanked it off the burner. "Just a minute!"

She put some ice cubes into the soup and got a plate of crackers ready for Willow while waiting for the soup to cool down.

"Crackers!" Sammy reached for Willow's crackers.

Willow threw Jess a pleading look.

"I'll get some more."

"Okay." Willow gave her brother a cracker. She took one for herself then turned back to the television.

Jess filled a huge bowl with crackers, gave it to Willow, then went back to the kitchen and started deleting negative comments until her finger hurt. Then she switched to a different finger.

"More soup!" Daisy called.

Now the previously scalding soup was cold. She microwaved it, took it out to her, then got back to deleting comments. Twelve hundred more to go.

Such a waste of her time, but what other choice did she have? She couldn't have them cluttering up her dashboard.

Then she realized what she really needed to do. She needed to amp up her search for the next baby.

Jess had lucked out with Sammy—snatching him from the park had been a stroke of fortune. The other three had all been meticulously planned out. She would need to do that again.

There wasn't any room for error. Not now.

ARGUE

Ava sipped the last of her diet pop and moved the empty foam cup to the tray of empty containers. Under the table, Braylon took her hand and squeezed. She squeezed back and smiled at him, hardly aware of Aiden and Emma across the table.

"Did you hear me?" Aiden asked.

Braylon gave her a crooked smile before turning to Aiden. "I was a little distracted. What'd you say?"

"I'm gonna get some more fries. You want anything?"

"No. I'm stuffed." Braylon rubbed his stomach. "Couldn't eat another bite if I wanted to."

Aiden turned to Ava. "How about you?"

She shook her head. If she really wanted to, she could probably eat more, but she wasn't hungry. Besides, she wanted to watch the scale.

"Come with me, anyway." Aiden rose and waved Braylon to come with him.

Braylon gave Ava an apologetic glance, let go of her hand, then followed him.

Emma sighed. "Boys are so lucky. They can eat and eat, and never gain a pound. Or if they do, they don't care."

"Right?" Ava peeked at her phone. More texts from Mason.

"What's up with your phone?"

Ava shoved it back into her purse. "What do you mean?"

"You know exactly what I mean." Emma pursed her lips. "Every time you check it, you get that look on your face."

"What look?"

"Like you've seen a ghost. What's up with that?"

Ava frowned.

"You don't have to tell me if it's too personal, but you can talk to me. I won't say anything to Braylon."

Her stomach twisted. "I'm not trying to keep anything from him… exactly."

Emma shrugged. "We all have secrets, and it's not like you're married. You don't have to tell him everything."

"I don't want to keep things from him," she snapped.

"It's not bad if you do. Probably healthy."

"You sound like a counselor." Unfortunately, Ava knew how they sounded from experience.

Emma sipped her drink. "I read a lot of advice columns."

Ava tapped her fingers on her knees and thought about Mason. She was protecting anyone she kept from knowing about him.

"I don't tell Aiden everything. A little mystery in relationships is a good thing." She glanced over at the boys, now heading back to the table, and lowered her voice. "It keeps them on their toes."

Aiden placed a bag on the table and pulled out two large containers of waffle fries. "You guys can help yourself. Or I can eat them all. I don't care." He laughed then stuffed one in his mouth before pulling out some dipping sauces.

Emma grabbed one and arched a brow at Ava.

They talked about the school's basketball team while Aiden ate most of the fries. Everyone else picked at them. Then Aiden and Emma had to go, so the two couples parted ways.

Braylon and Ava headed for the park, which had become their

typical hangout spot. It was several blocks from their houses, but because they always walked it felt a world away—as long as none of their siblings or parents were there.

"Why did Emma keep giving you those looks?" he asked.

"What looks?"

"You know."

"The girl wants to be a therapist."

"Huh?" Braylon's brows knit together.

"Never mind."

"Is everything okay?"

"Yeah. Why wouldn't it be?"

He shrugged. "You've been acting on edge a little lately. It's hard to explain. Is that history project getting to you?"

Relief washed through her. He thought it had to do with school. "Yeah, I can't quite figure out what to do with it. Everyone knows how hard Mr. Banks is. No matter what I do, he's going to find something wrong with it. He's ruined more four-point-oh averages than any other teacher alive. It's a proven fact."

"At least you don't have a four-point-oh to worry about."

She shoved him.

"I didn't mean it in a bad way!"

"Regardless, if my GPA drops, my dad's gonna be pissed. He cares a lot more about my grades than Mom ever did."

"Is that what's really bothering you?" His expression softened.

"What?"

"Your mom."

"I don't care about her," Ava said too quickly.

Braylon frowned. "It's okay to be mad or to hate her, you know."

"Now *you're* starting to sound like a counselor." She glared at him.

"Well, it *is* okay. She was engaged to the guy who shot up the school and kidnapped you. She was behind it. Knew everything."

"I said, shut up." She glared at him.

"You didn't say that."

Ava balled her fists. "I'm saying it now."

"At least you're finally showing some anger about her."

Fury pulsed through her veins. It took every ounce of her self-control not to hit him. "I don't want to talk about her!"

"Maybe you should."

"What do you think I do at the counseling sessions Dad drags me and my brother and sister to? We have to sit and talk about our feelings about the whole stupid thing for an hour."

"Does it help?"

"Does talking ever help?" Ava took a deep breath. "I thought we came here to hang out, but if you're going to insist on talking about my mom, I'm going home."

"Ava." He reached for her hand.

She yanked it away. "I'm serious. I don't want to talk about any of it. I'd rather enjoy just being here with you. It's a sunny Saturday. What else could I ask for?"

Her purse vibrated, meaning her phone was buzzing. Probably Mason sending another text. Her entire body tensed.

"Okay." Braylon's tone was soft. "What do you want to do? Join that game of tackle Frisbee over there?"

Ava shook her head. Her purse vibrated again. "Let's go climb that rock wall. The challenging side."

"That's what I'm talking about." Braylon put his arm around her, and they headed for the wall.

Guilt stung for taking her annoyance out on him and for not saying anything about Mason. But at least with Mason, she would find a way to get him off her back. The jerk had to want something, and it was just a matter of figuring out what, then sending him away.

The fewer people she involved, the better. No reason she couldn't handle him herself. Mason thought he was in control of the situation, but Ava was smarter. She could figure out a way to outwit him. She'd gotten away from his dad, and she could get away from him, too.

QUESTION

Nick's mind spun as he looked through images of marriage proposal ideas online. Every single one of them was more complicated than he could pull off. He was more of a candlelight dinner kind of a guy. And besides, he didn't want to wait for as long as it would take to pull off some of these plans—like renting a hot-air balloon, setting up a treasure hunt, or arranging it with a stage manager at the local theater and asking her in front of an audience.

He set his tablet down and closed his eyes, trying to think of something to make a dinner date proposal a little more creative. He could take her to one of the nearby lakes and ask her at sunset, if he could manage to swing it timewise. Sunsets were romantic. It could work. Plus, they could be engaged that night.

The front door swung open. "Hi, Daddy!"

Nick opened his eyes and turned toward his sweaty daughter. "Hi, Hanna. Having fun?"

"Yeah. We're playing tag and I'm thirsty." She ran to the kitchen.

"That's good. What do you think of going over to Ariana's house this evening?"

"I'd love it!" The fridge door slammed shut.

"Easy there, kiddo."

"I know."

Nick pulled out his phone and sent a quick text, asking Alex if it was okay to bring the kids over that evening.

Alex: U gonna propose?

Nick: I think so.

Alex: You think?

Nick: Still have to see if G's free tonight. Had to check with you first.

Alex: Go 4 it! Bring 'em over!

Nick: Thx.

Alex: Lemme know if u need anything else.

Nick: OK. I'll tell you the times soon.

Alex: K.

Nick's heart raced. It was really happening. All he had left was to schedule the date with Genevieve then make reservations at the restaurant. Hopefully, he could get into the one he wanted.

He drew in a deep breath before calling Genevieve. This conversation couldn't be over text.

"Hi, Nick." He could hear her beautiful smile as she answered.

He swallowed and tried to sound natural. "Hey, there. So, the kids have been begging me to get together with Tinsley and Ariana. Alex says they can watch the kids tonight. What do you say to an impromptu date?"

Nick cringed. He should've gone with a text. That sounded awful.

"I'd love to! It's been too long since we've had some alone time."

Relief washed through him. He silently thanked her for being so gracious toward his awkwardness. "Great. What time do you want me to pick you two up?"

"It'll be easier if we meet at the Nakano's house, don't you think? Not sure we can all fit into your Mustang."

"Right. Not sure what I was thinking." He did the math, trying to calculate dinner and proposing at the lake during sunset. "How does five sound?"

"Perfect. Where are we eating?"

He hesitated. If he said the restaurant he wanted and they were full, she'd be disappointed. "It's a surprise."

"Great. I love surprises."

"Good. I'll see you at five."

They said their goodbyes, then he called the restaurant, hoping against hope that they'd have room.

"You're in luck. We just had a cancellation for five-forty. Does that work for you?"

"It's perfect. Thank you."

Nick's hands shook as he texted Alex, letting him know what time four more kids would show up at his house. The next two hours went by in a blur as he prepared for the big night then rounded up his kids.

He was probably crazy for doing this on such short notice, but he'd been hanging onto the ring for what felt like ages. Besides, he wasn't getting any younger.

Tick, tock.

By the time he pulled up to the house, he could barely think straight. Ava and Hanna practically leaped out of the car. Parker, however, stopped and looked at Nick. "Don't we know anyone with boys? I'm surrounded by girls when we get together with these guys."

Nick nodded. "Understood. Next time, we'll set up a sleepover with one of your school buddies. Sound good?"

"Yeah, thanks. And Dad, good luck tonight. But you won't need it. She'll say yes. You can stop sweating."

He chuckled nervously. "Am I that obvious?"

"Totally. You need to chill or she's gonna know something's up. Just sayin'."

"Thanks for the tip. Oh, and if you need some guy time, hang out with Alex. I'm sure he'll understand."

"Okay." Parker headed toward the house.

Genevieve's car pulled in behind him.

Nick's stomach lurched. He was tempted to push off the proposal to a later date. But his kids knew what was going on. He couldn't chicken out now. Not when he'd had guns pointed at him, vicious dogs chasing him, and other far scarier things to face than asking the woman he loved to marry him.

He double-checked the ring in his pocket before opening his door and enveloping Genevieve in his arms. She smelled sweet, like spicy citrus. "It's so good to see you."

She met his gaze, her eyes shining. "And we're going on an actual date, no less."

His pulse drummed in his ears. He didn't trust his voice, so he planted his lips on hers then took her hand in his as they went to the house to say goodbye and thank Alex and Zoey for taking on a total of seven kids for the evening.

The drive to the restaurant went by in a blur as Nick went over how he would ask her to marry him.

Genevieve gasped. "We're eating at Christel's?"

He nodded and pulled up to the valet. "I hope that's okay with you. It's not like we get alone-time very often. I wanted to make the best of it."

"I don't know what to say."

He kissed her cheek. "You don't have to say anything." He got out, handed his key over, then opened Genevieve's door.

"Christel's. I can't believe it." She pressed on her red satin dress. "I should've worn something nicer."

"Nonsense. You're perfect."

She looked him over. "I should've known something was up when I saw you in a tie."

"This old thing?" he teased.

Once inside, he gave his name and they were seated immediately. At a table with a huge window overlooking the city. He couldn't have gotten better seats if he'd tried.

Genevieve's eyes widened. "This is amazing."

He smiled. "Only the best for you."

The meal went by in a blur and Nick's heart raced the whole time. Genevieve smiled a lot and seemed to genuinely enjoy herself. Good. That was what he wanted. He could barely taste his lobster or the decadent chocolate cake they shared.

Then it was time to leave. To go to the lake. The sun was closing in on the horizon. He would have just enough time to drive to the beach and pop the question to the backdrop of a multicolored sky.

Genevieve talked about the meal and the restaurant for the entirety of the short ride, giving Nick the opportunity to stay quiet. He was sure his tone would be shaky, giving away his plan.

"Where are we going?" she asked when he turned down the road to the beach.

"I thought we could watch the sunset over the water since we have a little time to ourselves."

"Really? This has to be the most romantic date ever."

He turned into the parking lot and didn't respond, his thundering heart making it hard to think. With any luck, she didn't notice the slight shake in his hands.

When he pulled into the spot, one of their favorite romantic songs played. He took advantage of the moment to hold her hand and take a deep breath. Being so nervous really pulled him from his element.

Genevieve leaned against him. "I love you."

"I love you, too." He tried to think of something more to add, but wanted to save it all for the proposal.

Once the song ended, he cut the ignition and they headed for the beach. Thankfully, it was mostly empty. There shouldn't be too many distractions.

Halfway to the shore, he tripped over his own foot. How cliché.

"Are you okay?" Was that a hint of teasing in her voice?

"Yeah, fine. You?"

She smiled, her eyes seeming to hold a laugh.

He relaxed a little. Finally. What was he so nervous about? This was Genevieve. She was beautiful and kind. They were made for each other. They were meant to be together. Of course she was going to say yes.

They made it to the water's edge, and Nick put his arm around her. She nestled close, fitting against him perfectly. Relaxing into him even further.

The sky was a bright orange blending with pink and purple to create a sight more breathtaking than he'd hoped for. And he needed to pop the question soon, before the colors disappeared.

Pulse racing, he took a step back and turned to her, gazing into her enchanting gray eyes. He drew in a deep breath. Silently told himself to chill.

She slid her hand in his and started to say something.

Nick cleared his throat. "Genevieve, I knew there was something special about you from the moment we met. I couldn't put my finger on it at first, and in fact, I tried to ignore that inkling altogether because we worked together and I was your captain. But it grew impossible to ignore the spark between us—the real reason we made such a good team. It's why you eventually left our precinct, even though there was some miscommunication involved. But time and space wasn't enough to keep us apart. Nothing can separate us, and I don't want to spend another day without seeing your gorgeous face, without touching you, without being close to you." He swallowed, then lowered himself to one knee and dug into his pocket.

Genevieve covered her mouth with both hands and tears shone in her eyes.

He pulled out the ring and studied her beauty. "What I'm trying to say is, will you marry me?"

She nodded and pulled her hands from her mouth. "Yes! Yes, of course I'll marry you!"

Relief washed through him. She'd said yes. He slid the ring on her finger—a perfect fit. Then she lowered herself to her knees. He kissed her deeply and passionately, savoring both her and the wild range of emotions raging through him.

SUSPICIOUS

A lex checked his phone. "They're almost here!"
Gasps, giggles, and shuffling sounded from the dark living room as the kids scurried to their hiding spots.

Shortly after Nick and Genevieve had dropped the kids off, Alex had taken them to the store to purchase some party supplies and decorations. Then they'd spent the rest of the evening getting ready for a surprise engagement party. He'd even invited his parents, sister and her family, and some of the guys from the station who Alex knew had the night off. To say that there were a lot of people hiding in the living room was an understatement. Only Zoey wasn't there. She had the babies in the apartment so the surprise part of the party didn't scare them.

A car drove on the street, slowing as it neared the house. Alex peeked through a blind to see the Mustang pulling up to the curb. "And they're here!"

People hushed each other and the house grew quiet—so quiet, Nick and Genevieve's footsteps could be heard from outside.

Ding-dong!

Alex couldn't hold back his grin as he opened the door. "It's the happy couple!"

They both beamed.

"Let me see the ring."

Genevieve held out her hand to show off the sparkling rock.

Alex let out a low whistle. "Nice. Well, come on in. The kids are watching a movie, so it's a little dark in here. You know how they like the theater experience to watch their favorite superheroes."

"That they do." Nick chuckled.

Alex stepped aside, letting them in. As soon as he closed the door, the lights came on, showing the balloons, streamers, and banners. Everyone jumped out, shouting their congratulations. Their kids enveloped them in hugs and the other guests surrounded the wide-eyed couple.

Once everything quieted a bit, Zoey emerged with the babies. She handed Laney to Alex and leaned against him. "They look so happy. I'm so excited for them."

"Me, too. This has been a long time coming."

"It sure has."

Ariana put on some music, then all the kids passed around cake and other snacks. Everyone mingled and enjoyed themselves.

Nick came over to Alex. "Thanks for the party. I certainly wasn't expecting all this."

"Everyone wanted to celebrate with you." Alex held up his glass of sparkling cider, and they tapped glasses. "To you and Genevieve."

"To love and good friends." Nick sipped his drink. "How'd you manage to pull all of this off with such short notice?"

"It was pretty easy with the kids. We've got some real party planners." He glanced over at Ariana and Ava, who were mixing a new batch of punch.

The party lasted about another hour before people started filtering out. Then only Nick and Genevieve remained. She glanced around. "Want us to stick around and help clean the mess?"

Alex shook his head. "You can't clean up after your own party. Leave the kids for a sleepover, and we'll all take care of this in the morning."

"Are you sure?" Nick asked.

"Of course. But you're bringing me a mint mocha when you come to pick the kids up."

Nick put his arm around Genevieve. "I think we can handle that."

The kids said goodbye to them, then Alex brought out the sleeping bags and really did put on a superhero movie. Though none of the kids managed to stay awake until the end.

Alex checked on Zoey, who was sound asleep with the twins in bed. He was tempted to crawl in, but instead grabbed his pillow to crash on the couch since the kids were in mixed company. Better safe than sorry. Nobody knew what could happen better than him, a guy who'd been an expectant dad at thirteen.

Even after settling into the couch his mind raced, not allowing him to sleep. He pulled out his phone and checked his email. Still no response from the mommy blogger, nor was there a notification of her responding to his blog comment.

No surprise there. Not that her lack of response would stop him. He just needed to send more messages until it was impossible to ignore him. Or until she blocked him, which was likely the more realistic option.

He checked his blog to see if there were any new comments on his post about the mommy blogger. His mouth dropped open when he saw how many comments there were. Not only that, but the post had been shared thousands of times on social media. Thousands.

A quick look at page views showed nearly a million views. His mind spun, hardly able to believe his eyes. Those were the numbers his dad was used to seeing, not him. His dad's blog was what had landed him his book deals which had gotten him on multiple bestseller lists.

Not that Alex expected, or even wanted, any of that. This was just a one-off. And it proved that he wasn't crazy for insisting something was wrong. Many others saw it, too.

It was just a matter of getting to the bottom of it and allowing the authorities to dole out justice. Hopefully they would find the boy alive and well, but his gut told him otherwise. If Connor was fine, he'd be in more recent pictures.

Alex read over the new blog comments and his eyelids grew heavy. But then as he got to the newer ones, he sat up. They were mentioning a new post from the blogger. An explanation.

What?

He fumbled over to her site and sure enough, there was a new post entitled *My Heartbreak*.

Alex's heart raced as the page loaded to finally reveal her side of the story.

THIS POST IS LONG OVERDUE. *I should apologize for taking so long, but I just can't. Especially since I feel forced to write this while my precious children are so horribly sick, as I mentioned in my last post.*

The reason I haven't said anything about my beloved Connor is because it hurts too much. I hate that I have to write about the whole situation now, but so many of you have had questions. Thank you for the kind private messages. They mean the world to me.

It pains me to admit that Connor doesn't live with us any longer. Behind the scenes, I've been dealing with a heart-wrenching custody battle. The father of my older three decided that he wanted to be involved in the life of only his son. Can you believe that? Just his son! But he's always been such a "man's man" that I shouldn't be surprised. You know the type—hunting, watching football, beating his chest, and everything that goes with it.

At any rate, the courts saw fit to allow poor Connor to be ripped from the only family he knows—his dad had always been nothing more than a myth before—and forced to live across the country with his father.

The whole ordeal has ripped me to shreds emotionally. Not just me— the girls, as well. They're as heartbroken as I am, but they don't understand why their brother is gone or why their dad only wanted Connor. Unfortunately, I can't really explain it to them. I don't want them to hate the justice system or to feel bad about their dad not wanting them just because they're girls, so what can I say? I just tell them how wonderful they are and how much I love them. If nothing else good comes from all of this, at least they will be secure in my commitment to them. I truly love my girls more than life itself, as I do all of my children. And that includes Connor, Sammy, and the baby growing inside of me at this very moment.

Some of you will want to know if I'm going to fight for custody again. I will, but not now. Both my funds and my emotions are depleted. Also, my lawyer says it's best that I wait. He even suggested I keep all this to myself, as posting about our situation might give my ex the upper hand in future custody battles. But you've all been curious, and I owed you, and my son, the courtesy of a post.

And if my ex ever does find this, here is a message for him—you may have won the battle, but you won't win the war. I will never give up on my children. Not ever.

Thank you again for all your support. A few people who I confided in before this post have suggested I start an online fundraiser for future legal fees. I'm not going to at this time, and I ask none of you do so on my behalf. I don't want anyone to think this is about the money. It's about Connor.

ALEX STARED in disbelief at his screen. He reread the post twice to make sure he'd read it right. Nothing added up. None of it.

He searched several keywords and found his suspicions proven right. Prior to this new post, there had been zero mentions of the children's father. No mention whatsoever of anything to do with custody or court. She carried on with life as normal, taking the kids on outings every day and posting about them.

If she had been dealing with a custody battle, that would have taken untold time and energy. There was no room in this woman's schedule for any of that, unless she'd been lying in the posts where she spelled out nearly every moment of their lives.

There was only one explanation, and it was that her post was exactly what she claimed it wasn't—a plea for sympathy. She wanted everyone to feel sorry for her and stop questioning her about the missing boy.

The post's comments indicated she had a strong following who believed her every word. But the real question was, how many comments was she withholding? How many were full of the same doubts Alex had?

More importantly, how would they get to the truth?

At least he had a platform. People would comment on his blog, where they could say their thoughts, unhindered and in the open.

But first, he would send another email to the mother. He would give her the chance to come clean before he posted another viral message to the world.

BLOCKING

J ess lay Sammy, fast asleep, in his crib and kissed his cheek before raising the side up. None of the kids had puked all day and now they were all sleeping like little angels. She fixed the covers around Sammy before going to the living room and collapsing onto the couch.

As much as she wanted to go to sleep—maybe she would sleep as well as the night before—she wanted to check her blog comments more. Her post had been so convincing that the first comments were filled with love and sympathy. She'd approved those right away. But it was no surprise that they were positive. The first readers were the ones who were subscribed to her blog. They got email notifications the moment her post went live.

The real question was if she had convinced the naysayers to stop asking her about Connor.

Her heart ached at the thought of him. She hadn't been able to stop the tears as she wrote the blog post. If she'd had her way, she'd never have mentioned him again on the blog. It really and truly hurt too much.

But not for the reason her followers now believed.

Jess's heart sunk when she saw the new flood of comments.

Most of them were still negative. Harsh. Unbelieving. They called her a liar and far worse.

Hands shaking, she not only deleted those posts but she blocked them from being able to comment again. She couldn't stop them from visiting her blog, but she could stop their vitriol in her online home.

Then she came to one that made her blood run cold. It was from Alexander again, and his message was short. It only read, *Check your email.*

She sat up taller. Like there was time for that. Time to worry about one guy out of thousands leaving her negativity. Sure, he seemed to mean business, but he was still just one person. He didn't know where or who she was.

Jess blocked him and moved onto the next comment, blocking that jerk, too. Her muscles relaxed. It helped to block the haters. Knowing that that they wouldn't be able to comment again. If only she could be there to see their faces when they tried to spew their loathing her way.

By the time she finally blocked all of them, her body cried out for sleep again. Her throat even hurt a little, almost as though she'd been screaming.

Or worse, she was getting sick. No! There was no time for that. The kids were finally starting to feel better. She needed to get them out and about, to go somewhere fun and get lots of pictures. Write up a brilliant blog post and convince others they were all moving on despite Connor's absence. Perhaps come up with some kind of proof that he was alive and well. Mention a phone call, maybe. Yeah, that was good. And if people didn't buy it, that would give her time to think of something else.

Jess pulled herself up from the chair, went into the kitchen, and took every vitamin she could find. Getting sick wasn't an option. Not now. Once things calmed down, she could give in to a virus.

She brushed her teeth then flopped onto her bed, barely taking the time to pull her covers over her. Sleep fog was just starting to take over when her phone beeped. She'd forgotten to silence it.

Groaning, she felt around for the device. It beeped again. Had to be just out of reach. Maybe it would stay quiet after this and let her sleep.

It beeped again.

She sat up, annoyance coursing through her body. Where'd she put it? As tired as she was, she couldn't even remember putting it down. It beeped again. She found it on her nightstand.

Just as she was moving the bar over to silence it, she read part of a notification on the screen. It was from one of her social media profiles. From the looks of it, someone had posted on her wall that she was a child killer.

All fatigue fled. Her entire body went cold. The phone shook in her hands. She needed to change her profile settings immediately. People couldn't post that stuff on her wall! Her followers would see that.

Jess's stomach lurched as she unlocked the phone and clicked on the first notification. A stream of vile posts filled her wall. She'd be lucky to get any sleep from the looks of it.

By the time she'd removed all the posts and changed her settings to prevent anyone from posting on her wall, a full hour had passed. And she still had several more social media sites to check.

Why were bloggers expected to be active everywhere? She cursed the whole setup as she checked the next site. Not as many posts, but still a huge mess to clean up and more settings to change. This one would be harder because anyone could tag her in their own postings, and from the looks of it, every single hater was doing just that. They couldn't tag her if she blocked them, so she got busy blocking as many as she could.

Once she'd finally calmed that storm, light was starting to come up in the sky. Not only that, but her throat was hurting worse than before.

Why did people have to be so mean? Couldn't they see she was just a single mom trying to take care of her kids? They could so easily direct their anger at someone else. Someone who was actually trying to do harm in the world. She just wanted to give her kids a good life. Nothing more, nothing less.

She absolutely had to get some sleep. It wouldn't be much after having to block so many posts and comments, but now people couldn't spew their theories on her blog or any of her profiles. She could carry on, focusing only on the people who supported her. And there were plenty of them. They were the ones who mattered.

Jess started to close her screen when a new notification popped up. She had a new email from that Alexander guy.

He could wait. The whole world could wait until she got some sleep. But even then, they would still have to wait. Once she woke up, she was going to find her next baby. That would be the perfect distraction from this whole mess.

HASHTAG

Alex moved the bacon from the frying pan to a plate and checked his phone again. Still nothing from the mommy blogger, other than the fact that she'd removed scathing accusations from her social media profiles. An innocent person would simply state the truth, put out the fire. Not try to hide any and all condemning evidence.

"You want me to take over the cooking?" Zoey bounced Laney. "So you can keep checking your phone."

He shoved his phone into his back pocket and checked the cinnamon rolls in the oven. "No, I've got this. Those kids still sleeping?"

Zoey nodded. "Except for Hanna. She's watching cartoons on my tablet."

Alex flipped over the omelet. "I don't know about Ava and Parker, but Ari would sleep until noon if she could."

"Sounds like someone else I know." Zoey winked.

"Who? Me? My schedule's off because of the night shift."

"I mean when we were teenagers. You acted like sleeping in was an Olympic sport."

"Did I?"

She snorted.

He checked the omelet. "I wish I could sleep that much again, but it'll get better as the twins get older."

Zoey glanced outside, where her parents were busy with their garden. "Or we'll get used to rising early and keep it up as we age."

Alex yawned. "I can't imagine that. I'd sleep in if I could."

They teased each other for a few minutes before the kids came into the kitchen. Hanna bounced in, saying how great the food smelled. The others trudged in, rubbing their eyes and bemoaning the early morning hours.

"It's almost ten," Alex pointed out.

Hanna skipped over. "Can I help?"

He glanced around, trying to figure out what would be safe.

"I help Dad cook all the time."

Alex handed her a packet of frosting. "You can put this on the cinnamon rolls."

"Easy peasy, lemon squeezy."

"Don't put more on the one you're going to claim." Parker reached for the coffee pot.

Alex arched a brow. "Does your dad let you drink coffee?"

"Yeah."

Ariana's mouth dropped open. "Not fair."

"He does?" Alex turned to Ava.

She nodded. "But he puts so much creamer in, it's not really coffee."

"There you go." Alex glanced at Ari before splitting the omelet into five pieces and giving a portion to each of the kids.

They scarfed down the food in a fraction of the time it took Alex to make it, then scattered out of the kitchen.

Before long, Nick and Genevieve arrived to pick up their kids. Once they left, Zoey handed Laney to Alex. "Can you watch the babies for a while? I promised Ari I'd take her to the store for some girl stuff."

Alex's stomach knotted. "I don't even want to know."

Zoey kissed his cheek. "It's all part of life. I won't be gone long."

"Take all the time you need. Is Zander still sleeping?"

She nodded. "Just checked the monitor. I think he's fighting something off. His nose was runny last night."

"I'll keep an eye on that." He gave her a quick kiss before heading to the apartment. Laney squirmed to get out of his hold, so he set her on the floor where they had gates blocking off their play area, though they weren't even scooting yet.

He checked on Zander, who was snoring because of a crusty nose but was otherwise fine, then he sat at his desk where he had a clear view of Laney trying to suck on a block so big it would never fit into her mouth.

Alex responded to some blog comments before opening his email. Nothing from the mommy blogger. She didn't have any new posts up yet, either. Maybe she'd been too busy trying to hide the truth that she hadn't been able to take her remaining kids anywhere. It made perfect sense.

He tapped his finger on the desk and considered writing another post. The woman had had plenty of time to respond to his emails. She was ignoring him just like all the comments on her blog.

The woman clearly had something to hide. Her story about the custody battle was nothing but fiction. She was trying to cover her tracks, hiding whatever happened to that little boy.

It was time to really put on the pressure. His first post had gone viral. A new one had the potential to do even better because of the momentum of the first one.

Alex refreshed his email, and still seeing nothing from the blogger, he started a new post. His fingers flew across the keyboard as he summarized the previous post then updated his readers on the new developments.

After reading it over, it seemed to be missing something. Not any details—he'd gone over those in painstaking detail. No, the post needed some… what? Oomph. That was exactly what it needed. But what would provide the oomph?

He noticed Laney had fallen asleep on the blanket she was sprawled across. He got up and placed her in her crib, his mind racing for the answer. What was his post lacking? It needed just a little something to give it more viral power.

Zander coughed and let out a cry. Alex picked him up, changed him, fed him—all the while trying to figure it out.

Then, just as Zander spit up all over the front of his shirt, Alex figured it out.

He needed a hashtag. One that would not only be catchy, but would provide a way for people to find each other's posts and comments all over the various platforms. It would make every post all the more shareable.

Zander squirmed to be let down, so Alex put him on the blanket. He grabbed the same block his twin had been playing with and tried to put it in his mouth.

Alex watched him, his mind mulling over potential hashtags. Then one came that gave him pause. Mommy Blogger Mayhem. It was a little long, but it was catchy and would be easy to remember. Hopefully people could spell mayhem. He found spelling errors all over the web, and he wasn't even a grammar Nazi.

If it got too confusing, people could shorten it. It could evolve into MBM if that wasn't being used for anything else. It could work. It would work.

He turned back to his laptop filled with a renewed determination. At the end of his blog post title, he added the hashtag. That way anytime someone shared the post, they would also share the hashtag.

Excitement drumming through him, he proofread the post before publishing it. Then he shared the link all over social media using the hashtag.

#MommyBloggerMayhem. It was perfect.

With any luck, soon it would be trending. It would get the

word out to enough people that someone would recognize her and come forward with the truth. Or at least something that would point to the truth.

The woman would be forced to come clean. And if she didn't, enough evidence would surface to convict her of any wrongdoing.

FIGHT

"Would you stop checking your phone?"

Ava glanced across the table at Dad. They were having lunch with Genevieve and Tinsley to celebrate the engagement, and it was almost like Mason knew because he wouldn't stop texting her.

Maybe he did know. Blood drained from her face.

Genevieve smiled at Ava. "It's okay. Does Braylon miss you?"

Ava forced a smile. "Yeah."

"We should've invited him."

"No." Dad's brows furrowed into one as he glared at Ava. "This is family time. Nobody else is glued to the phone."

"You're right. I'll put it away." She silenced it and returned it to her purse.

Parker's mouth fell open dramatically. "You just admitted Dad's right?"

She narrowed her eyes, willing herself to shoot him with death rays.

The conversation moved to the wedding. Ava tried to shove Mason's texts from her mind and channeled her excitement. Even though she was distracted and worried, she really was happy that

Dad and Genevieve were getting married. It was about time he found happiness. He'd been so miserable before Genevieve showed up.

They discussed dates, locations, and how to have each of the kids involved.

Ava put her fork down and looked at Genevieve. "It should all be about what you want." She didn't want to point out the obvious —that it was her first wedding and Dad's second. He'd already been through all of this, so Genevieve doubly deserved to have the wedding of her dreams.

Genevieve beamed. "That means so much, but it's not just about your dad and me. The five of us are becoming a family. I want *that* to be the focus."

Ava nodded. "What have you always pictured your wedding to be like?"

She chuckled. "You know, I never really put much thought into it. Was never really sure I'd marry."

"Really?" Ava leaned forward.

"It's true. I've been career-focused for so long, and I wasn't sure anyone would want to put up with an officer's schedule."

Ava knew exactly what she meant. Her mom used to complain about Dad's schedule. All. The. Time. "Well, nobody gets it like Dad."

Genevieve and Dad exchanged a sweet glance.

Parker rolled his eyes and whispered, "Suck up."

Ava kicked him under the table. She'd deal with the jerk at home. This wasn't the time for him to be a jerk.

Genevieve turned to Hanna. "What do you think?"

She set her shake down. "I want to be a flower girl."

"I would love that, and I bet you'll be the best there ever was."

Dad turned to Tinsley. "And how are you feeling?"

She smiled wider than Ava had ever seen. "I can't wait to have a dad and brothers and sisters. It'll be a whole family. Are you going to adopt me, too?"

A warmth spread through Ava. Tinsley was one of the quietest people she'd ever met, even though she'd come so far from when they'd first met her and she never spoke a word because of her psychotic upbringing. Her real parents were actual crazy-pants. Between what her dad and Genevieve had told them and what little Tinsley had shared, it made everything Ava had been through feel like nothing.

Dad reached across the table and put his hand on hers. "Nothing would make me happier."

Parker muttered something under his breath.

Ava kicked him again and shot him a death glare. He returned it with one of his own. She was definitely going to have it out with him once they left. There were times to be selfish, and this wasn't one of them. She mouthed, "Shut it."

He mouthed, "Make me."

Her blood boiled, but she wasn't going to let him ruin this meal celebrating the engagement. She took a deep breath and looked away from him. Luckily, nobody else seemed to notice him. Either that or they were doing a good job of ignoring him.

The waiter came and dropped off the check. Before long, they were heading to the cars.

"Can I ride with Genevieve?" Hanna asked.

Ava turned to Parker. "What's up your butt?"

His eyes narrowed. "Leave me alone."

"We're supposed to be celebrating with Dad and Genevieve. Instead, you're making it about you."

"Trust me, if I was making it about me, you'd know it."

"That was you holding back?"

Parker shoved her.

She pushed him. "Stop!"

He stuck his foot in front of her ankle. Before Ava could react, she flew forward. The pavement was coming at her fast. She put out her arms to protect her face and head. The impact burned up and down her arms. Pain shot through one knee and a hip. Her head bumped the curb at the same moment her purse flew from her hand and bounced, spilling the contents as it went.

Everyone spoke at once.

Ava scrambled to her feet, her face burning from embarrassment, and she dusted herself off. Blood, dirt, and pebbles stuck to the scrapes on her arms. Her new jeans were ripped, and not in a way that looked stylish. Her head throbbed where it had hit the curb.

Parker stood there as smug as could be. It was enough to make her not care about keeping the peace anymore. She lunged for him, but just before she could inflict pain, Dad grabbed her.

"Let's get you cleaned up."

"He did that on purpose!"

"We'll get to the bottom of this at home." He turned to Parker. "Help pick up your sister's things."

"No."

"No?" Dad let go of Ava.

"You heard me."

Hanna picked up Ava's purse. "I'll get the stuff." She picked up a tube of lipstick and put it inside.

Dad stepped so close to Parker that their noses almost touched. "You'd better rethink your attitude, and quickly. Or there will be consequences."

"Whatever."

Hanna handed Ava her cell phone. "Mason texted you?"

Blood drained from her body.

Dad whipped around. "What?"

Parker smirked. "She's been getting them for a while."

"How did you know?" Ava demanded.

He folded his arms. "Your password couldn't have been easier to figure out."

She lunged for him, ready to permanently remove his smug expression.

Dad turned back toward Parker. "You *knew* about this?"

Parker's grin faded.

Good.

"You knew that dangerous kid was texting your sister and you didn't tell me?" Spittle flew from Dad's mouth.

"I—"

"You're grounded until further notice." He spun back toward Ava. "You both have some serious explaining to do as soon as we get home."

Genevieve put her hand on Dad's arm. "I can take Hanna and Tinsley somewhere for a while, then bring Hanna back when you're ready."

Dad took a deep breath. "I'd appreciate that. I need to have a serious talk with these two right now."

Ava's stomach flip-flopped.

BLINDSIDED

Nick paced the living room, hardly able to look at his two oldest children. He took deep breaths and considered his wording carefully. They would all regret it if he said what he felt like saying.

He stopped pacing and looked at Ava on the couch and Parker on the recliner. "I don't even know where to start!"

Ava raised her road-rashed arms. "You could start with him tripping me on purpose. I was telling him to—"

"She's the one who's been texting with Mason!" Parker pointed at his sister.

"Enough! You two couldn't get along for just one day? All I wanted was a nice afternoon to celebrate the engagement!"

"He's the one who—"

"Stop!" Nick held up a hand. "I don't want to hear any blaming. None."

Ava glared at Parker.

Parker gave her an obscene gesture.

"What is going on with you two? Stop!"

Ava opened her mouth, but then closed it.

"What?" Nick demanded.

"You said you didn't want blaming. I can't tell you what happened without blaming him."

Nick drew in a deep breath and went back to pacing. "Do you really think Genevieve is going to want to join this family when you kids pull stunts like this?"

Neither responded.

"Or is that what you want?" He stopped cold and met the gaze of both kids.

Ava's eyes shone. "*I* want you two to get married." Her mouth contorted like she was struggling not to say more.

Nick turned to his son. "And you?"

"No comment."

"Excuse me?"

"I said, no comment."

Nick counted silently before responding. "I heard you. What exactly do you mean? And don't say 'no comment' again unless you want to find out what military school is like."

His mouth dropped open. "You can't be serious."

"Don't test me. Not today."

Parker didn't respond.

Nick took a step closer. "I said, tell me exactly what you mean by 'no comment.'"

They stared each other down before Parker finally spoke. "After everything we've been through, you really expect us to be happy about this?"

"That doesn't answer my question."

"Our mom is in jail for life and you expect us to act like Genevieve is our new mom. She's not a replacement for Mom."

"I never expected her to be! She's an addition to our life—a positive one, at that. But I never once told any of you to forget about your mother *or* that Genevieve would replace her. I'm not blind or stupid, Parker. But do you know what else?"

"What?" Parker's tone had less of an edge to it.

"We're lucky that Genevieve wants to be a part of our lives.

She knows full well what baggage we have, and she still loves us. Not just me, but all three of you. Do you think for a moment I'd marry her if it was any other way? Do you?"

Parker's knuckles turned white.

"You kids are my priority. So is Genevieve, but she wouldn't be if you weren't important to her. You might've noticed how long I waited after your mother left me before I dated. *She* may not care how her choice in a life partner affects you, but I do. I understand you have to deal with the consequences of her actions, but don't take it out on me or Genevieve."

"Or me," Ava muttered.

"None of us deserves it," Nick continued. "You can talk to the counselor more if you want, and I'm always here to talk, but don't ever pull a stunt like that again. Do you understand?"

Parker's mouth formed a straight line.

"Do you understand?" Nick repeated.

"Yes."

"Good. If you have a problem or concern, *talk* to me about it. We can work out a solution. Don't hide things from me and don't act out. I'd expect that from a toddler, not you."

Parker nodded, his expression tight.

"If a member of our family is in danger, tell me! I really don't appreciate you keeping Mason's texts from me. He's dangerous— to all of us! The kid has mental problems, and he probably blames us for his parents being in jail." Despite the divorce, despite being engaged to Genevieve, it still made him a little sick to acknowledge Corrine as Mason's mother. He still couldn't get over how blind he'd been to miss something so major like that.

Nick paced again, his mind racing. He probably shouldn't have been surprised to find out that Mason had been trying to contact Ava. The psychotic little turd was obsessed with her, despite finding out that they were half-siblings.

He turned to Ava. "When did he start texting you?"

She looked away. "A while ago."

"When is a while ago?"

Parker snickered.

Nick glared at him. "Military school is not an empty threat."

Parker's expression stiffened.

Nick turned back to Ava. "You were saying?"

She played with the rip in her jeans. "I don't know when it started. I'd have to look at my phone, which you took away."

"Who else knows? Does Braylon?"

Ava shook her head. "I haven't told him."

Relief washed through Nick. He'd hate to have to drag Braylon into this mess. He was a nice kid, and Nick trusted him. This proved his instincts were still on target. "Glad to hear it. It's just you two?"

They both nodded.

Nick took a deep breath. "Does Mason know where we live?"

Ava sighed. "He knows we're in Washington."

"But he doesn't have our address? Know what school you go to?"

Ava shook her head.

"But he has your cell phone number."

"Yeah."

"How'd he get that?"

She shrugged.

Nick wanted to punch something. He counted to ten silently. Twice. "Do you know where he is?"

"Somewhere in Idaho."

"Idaho?" Nick exploded. "How'd he get across the country?"

"Probably drove."

He sat on the coffee table, knee-to-knee with Ava. "Tell me everything."

She sighed. "You have my phone. You can read it for yourself."

"I want to hear it from you."

Ava glared at Parker.

"Don't look at me."

Nick turned to his son. "Go to your room and do homework. Nothing else. Just homework. If you're tempted to get online, look up military schools."

Parker narrowed his eyes at his sister then headed to the hall.

"Homework only!"

"Got it, Dad." He disappeared around the corner.

Nick faced his oldest. "What does Mason text you about?"

"Stupid stuff."

"Meaning?"

She continued playing with the hole in her pants. "Tells me where he's living. For a long time, it was Kansas with his girlfriend. Then suddenly, it was Idaho."

Nick rubbed his temples. "You realize he's headed this way?"

"Yeah."

"Why didn't you tell me?"

"Because I had it under control."

Nick bit his tongue and drew in a deep breath. "You had it under control?"

She nodded. "It seemed like he wanted ties with his family. At least at first. I mean, he has a girlfriend. So, obviously, he's moved on from his obsession with me. Or at least I thought he had. Then he said he was in Idaho."

"And you still didn't think to tell me?"

She chewed on her lower lip. "I didn't want to worry you."

"Worrying about you is my job! And as police captain, I have the resources to deal with this. I can't believe you thought you could handle it on your own!"

"Well, I did a pretty good job. He hasn't shown up here. He's not anywhere near any of us. And besides, for all we know, he's headed this way to see Mom and Dave."

"I doubt that's the *only* reason he's so close."

Ava frowned.

Nick sat next to her. "Look, I don't want to take your phone away, but at the same time, I need to know that I can trust you. Will you tell me when he contacts you?"

"Yes."

"Okay." He handed the phone to her. "Let's look over Mason's texts together."

Pink colored her cheeks. "Just know that the only reason I said anything at all to him was because I wanted to keep my enemy close. I don't know if that makes sense to you, but that's what I was doing. Some of it might look like friends talking, but it's not. I know better than that. Really, I do."

Nick kissed the top of her head. "I believe you. Now, let's have a look."

TRENDING

A lex couldn't keep the smile off his face. His hashtag was actually trending on two of the social media sites. His two latest blog posts had more comments than any others.

He'd successfully brought light to the unusual situation. People were talking, and most everyone believed Connor was either in danger or dead. Alex hoped for the first, but given how long it had been and statistics, there was no denying the unlikelihood of it. The best anyone could realistically hope for was that the truth would come out and all guilty parties would be caught.

Zoey sat next to him and gave him a quizzical glance. "What are you so happy about?"

"My hashtag is trending."

She gave him a high-five. "You think it'll help find her?"

"It has to. There are hundreds of people discussing her blog, dissecting post after post. A guy in Oregon swears he recognizes one of the places she took the kids since Connor's disappearance."

"And she's not responding to any of it?"

"Not even close. She's blocked quite a few of us from commenting on her blog and from seeing her social media profiles."

"Does she really think that's enough? I mean, if she's hiding something about her son being hurt or worse..." Zoey shuddered.

"Doesn't matter what she thinks. She can run, but she can't hide forever. The truth is going to come out one way or another."

"What if she decides to quit blogging? Then there won't be any new clues to go on."

"True. But from what I've gathered, it's her only source of income. She has ads, sponsored posts, she reviews products—the whole shebang. Without another source of funds, she has to keep blogging."

Zoey lifted an eyebrow. "Can't she just start a new blog? Anonymously?"

"She *could*. But it'd be unlikely. Too much work to start over from scratch. She's got a good thing going for herself. Looks like she's making some good money from this one."

"But if everyone thinks she hurt that boy, wouldn't that hurt her bottom line?"

He frowned. "Unfortunately, it's probably helping. She's probably getting more pageviews than ever. She really has the site monetized well."

"Well, once she's in jail, it won't do her a bit of good."

"That's true." He gave her a kiss. "You mind if I call Nick? Or do you need help with the babies?"

"Call him. It's all good." She squeezed his hand and walked over to check on the babies, who were fascinated with a squeaky ball.

Alex grabbed his phone then settled on his bed and called Nick.

"Hey." Nick didn't sound himself.

"Something wrong?" Alex asked.

"That obvious?"

"Yeah. I thought you'd be walking on air."

"I *was*."

Alex waited for Nick to continue, but he didn't. "Don't tell me there's trouble in paradise already."

"No. My kids. The older two. No surprise there, is it?"

"Sorry to hear that. They having trouble blending the two families?"

Nick sighed. "I wish that was all it was. No, it's Mason. He's been texting Ava, and neither she nor Parker bothered to mention it to me."

"What?" Alex's mind spun. Mason was nothing but trouble for Ava, or for any of them. He glanced over at the babies, one of whom was related to Mason—a thought Alex pushed out of his mind every time it entered. As far as anyone was concerned, Alex was both Laney and Zander's dad. His name was on both certificates. No questions were asked because he and Zoey were married at the time. It wasn't like anyone asked for a blood test.

But the genetics were an entirely different story. Thanks to Dave abducting and abusing Zoey.

Alex snapped his attention back to the phone conversation. "Why has he been texting her?"

Zoey glanced over at him with furrowed brows. The last thing he wanted was to worry her, even though it was unlikely Mason had any idea about the twins. He got up and went into the empty backyard.

"He's headed our way," Nick said. "Might already be in the state. If not yet, then soon."

Alex took a deep breath and tried to calm himself. "What does he want?"

"My daughter!"

"Even though they're brother and sister?"

"*Half*," Nick corrected. "It's Parker who could be Mason's full sibling."

"Maybe you should get that paternity test. Set your mind at ease."

"Or have my world crushed!"

Alex paced. "At least you'd know. I think it's the not knowing that's harder on you."

"I don't care about genetics. He's my son!"

"I get it. Believe me."

"Right. I know. What am I supposed to do? Tell him and then do the test? Secretly take the test and hope it comes out in my favor? Or wait and see what the test results are, and then tell him if it's bad news?"

Alex pulled on his hair. "I'm facing the same dilemma, Nick. You know what conclusion I've come to?"

"What?"

"There is no right answer. It's a horrible situation and Dave is a horrible person to have done this. But the kids deserve to know the truth. Eventually, it could be a matter of safety. They're going to need to know their medical histories."

"I don't want to talk about this right now. What did you call about?"

"It's not important."

"Are you sure?"

"Yeah. We can talk about it later. Just figure out what's going on with Mason, and keep Ava safe."

"I'll let you know if I learn anything new, but I really don't think you have anything to worry about. I'm sure he has no clue about Zander being his brother."

Alex clenched his jaw. "He's not the one I'm worried about finding out."

"The good news is that Dave is never getting out of prison. He can't attempt to go after custody of either of our boys."

"At least you have a chance of your son actually being yours. You should find out and stop worrying. Maybe Corrine was actually telling the truth that one time."

"I'm not going to hold my breath. Talk to you later, Alex."

"Later." Alex ended the call and leaned against a pine tree, his mind reeling. For the last year, nobody had a clue where Mason was, and now the kid shows up? Some timing.

Alex had fallen in love with both babies the moment he saw them. He'd known that Zander was baby B—Dave's biological child—but he hadn't allowed that to get in the way of anything. Alex had already promised Zoey he would raise them both as his. They'd had a quick wedding in order to secure Alex's name on the birth certificates.

He *was* Zander's dad in every other sense of the word. Alex was raising him, loving him, providing for him, giving him a family. Sure, one day, he would have to come clean. Tell him the truth—hard as that would be. But he would be the first to know, outside of Zoey, Alex, and Nick.

It wasn't something he and Zoey had wanted to broadcast to the world, especially before the court trial. It was bad enough that she had to get on the stand and relive her ordeal, the last thing either of them wanted was to bring up the fact that her abuser had also fathered one of her children.

Luckily, it had barely come up. Because she'd been carrying two babies and it was her second pregnancy, she looked much further along than she'd actually been. It had been assumed she had already been pregnant when kidnapped. Zoey never corrected anyone and nobody questioned it. And considering that Dave had shot up a school, blown it up, and killed some people, those violations had been the focus of the trial. Not the pregnancy of a married woman who looked like she'd already been expecting at the time of the ordeal.

Alex and Nick had both been annoyed that more focus hadn't been on him abducting Zoey and Ava, but they were relieved that neither had to endure days of testifying. The short time of questioning had been traumatic enough for both of them, but it could've been so much worse.

Now the question was if he should tell Zoey that Mason was heading their way. She'd been so happy recently, he didn't want to

throw a wrench in her progress by potentially upsetting her again. But it wasn't like Dave had escaped prison. It was his son, a young guy who had no clue Zander was his half-brother.

Alex's stomach knotted. As much as he hated it, he knew what he had to do.

WRECK

Alex drew in a deep breath. His mind flooded with reasons—excuses—not to tell Zoey about Mason being close by. It wasn't going to affect them. Mason was only in the area to see Ava. Maybe his parents. The kid had no idea about Zander and probably wouldn't care. Telling Zoey would only stress her out. Maybe set her back, send her back to counseling.

But it wasn't up to him to keep the truth from her. She deserved to know what was going on, even if it didn't directly affect her or Zander. She was smart and capable and would know what to do.

"You look like you have the weight of the world on your shoulders."

Alex jumped at her voice.

She rubbed his shoulders. "I thought you were going to take a nap before heading into work."

He glanced at the time and his pulse raced, drummed in his ear. "I still have time, but I have to tell you something."

She tilted her head. "What?"

Alex took a deep breath and held it for a moment. "Nick found out Mason's in the area."

Zoey's eyes widened. "Mason? As in, Dave's son?"

"Yeah. He wants to see Ava."

Her eyes flitted as she took in the news. "What's Nick doing about it?"

"Trying to protect her as best he can."

"But he assaulted her. Don't they have a restraining order?"

Alex shook his head. "Ava swears nothing happened, that she got away before Mason had a chance to do anything. She won't press any charges."

"What about him coming here? That has to be grounds for an order."

"I think he has to do something to her first. I'm not all that familiar with restraining orders. The grounds for one is more of a legal matter. The ones I've dealt with were already set in place."

Zoey twisted a strand of hair around her finger and looked away. "Chances are, Mason won't have any interest in us. Even if he knew about Zander, I doubt he'd care. He doesn't seem to care about Parker or Hanna. Just Ava, right?"

Alex frowned. "Fixated would be a better word, but yes."

"Let him know if he's worried about her, she can stay with us until this calms down."

He gave her a double-take. "Really? You're not worried about him coming here?"

She shook her head no. "Mason's not going to have any interest in us, and he'd have a harder time tracking her down here. As long as you're okay with it, I think we should let Nick know that her staying here is an option."

"I'll let him know. But you can keep thinking about it while I sleep."

"I won't change my mind." She kissed him. "Have sweet dreams."

Alex got ready for bed and it seemed as soon as his head hit the pillow, his alarm woke him. He turned it off, yawned, and stretched. Then he checked the time. Sure enough, it was time to get ready for work. Zoey and the twins were sound asleep next to him. He gave each one of them a light kiss before getting ready and heading out.

It was a double-mocha kind of a night, so he stopped at his favorite coffee stand.

"How are those twins?" asked the barista as she made the drink.

"Getting bigger every day."

"They'll be going to college before you know it," she teased.

"Ugh. Don't remind me. My oldest definitely will."

"Is she in high school already?"

"Stop." Alex laughed.

"Just teasing." She told him the total, and he gave her a generous tip.

When he got to work, everything was pretty quiet. Most everyone was busy with office work, which didn't often happen. Not on his shift, anyway. After some small talk, he hit his paperwork that had piled up over the weekend. Wouldn't be long before he was called out for something—bar brawl, holdup, drug deal. Dull moments never seemed to last long.

After a while, Detective Sanchez stopped by his desk. "Ready to go on patrol?"

"Yes." He got up and stretched. "Been sitting too long."

"Sometimes quiet nights are nice."

"Yeah, the paperwork's a dream." He finished his mocha then tossed it into a can.

She snickered. "Well, after a busy weekend, I'd have to say it's an appreciated break."

They made their way to a cruiser then headed for a shadier part of town. Radio chatter reported complaints of cars racing down a residential street.

Detective Sanchez responded, letting them know she and Alex would check it out. They weren't far, and Alex didn't mention that he'd raced his first car down that very street numerous times in the past. It was a long, straight shot but curved sharply near the end and would be dangerous if a driver couldn't stop in time.

As they neared the road, Sanchez turned on the lights but not the sirens. Teens and young twenty-somethings ran in all directions. Two cars lined up next to each other, burned rubber, then sped down the street.

The cruiser raced after them, sirens now blaring. Neither car slowed, much less stopped. They were neck and neck, going forty then fifty. Sixty. Seventy. Seventy-five.

Beads of sweat broke out on Alex's forehead. The cars were nearing the dangerous curve, but instead of slowing, they were continuing to gain speed.

Sanchez eased off the gas. The other two cars continued increasing their speed. Alex's heart thundered. It would be dangerous enough for one car to attempt the curve, but two would be reckless. Deadly. Even at Alex's stupidest, he'd have never gone around that corner over thirty-five miles an hour.

The cars in front of them were nearing ninety.

One car slowed. The other didn't. Traveling at least ninety, the white Acura rounded the corner. Or tried to.

The crunching metal could be heard over the sirens. Car parts sprayed out like water from a hose.

Alex grimaced. It was going to be bad. Really bad.

The other car continued around the corner. Didn't slow. Drove right past the mangled vehicle.

As they approached, Alex snapped a picture of the car, zooming in on the license plate, just before it disappeared from sight. The cruiser's camera would have probably gotten video, but he wasn't taking any chances.

He radioed in a description of the car with its plates and updated the operator on the crash. Fire exploded, enveloping the Acura.

Without a word, he and Sanchez raced to the flames. Alex had a small fire extinguisher ready. Hopefully it would be enough to get the driver out. He sprayed the fire as Sanchez flung open the door.

She turned to him. "There's a passenger!"

Everything went by in a blur as they struggled to free both the young driver and passenger from the inflamed vehicle. Sanchez started CPR on the male driver. The girl Alex pulled out was breathing but not responsive. He carefully carried her to the other side of the street, worried the fire would get worse. So far, it was in the hood only. Not near the gas tank. Yet.

Sirens sounded. Fire trucks and an ambulance arrived. The firefighters quickly put out the blaze while the medics took the girl from Alex.

The paramedics tried to revive the driver, but after five minutes he was declared dead.

It felt like a punch to the gut. Given how many times Alex had raced the same road, that could've been him years earlier. Who was to say that his pride wouldn't have gotten in his way just once, and he might've tried that curve.

Why had he been so lucky?

The ambulance sped off with the passenger, and the coroner's van left with the deceased driver inside. Residents now crowded around the street, snapping pictures.

Alex had to pull himself together. He could wallow in survivor's guilt later. For now, someone needed to move the onlookers and set up police tape to keep them away from the wreckage.

It was going to be one long night.

NEAR

Ava rubbed her arm and winced. She'd worn long sleeves to school to cover her wounds, but she hadn't anticipated her skin catching on the fabric every time she moved.

She'd make Parker pay. Shove *him* down. Give him a taste of his own medicine. Jerk.

"How are you feeling?"

Ava slammed her locker shut and smiled weakly at Braylon. "Other than wanting to skin my brother's arms?"

"Want me to take care of him?"

She shook her head. "It's between me and him."

"I don't mind. Parker won't ever mess with you again after I'm done with him."

"No, I need to deal with him. But thanks."

Braylon looked at her arms. "Still refuse to show me?"

"My arms are gross."

"Blood is cool."

"And boys are weird." The warning bell rang. "We'd better go."

He put his arm around her, and they headed for their history class. "You know, I can talk to him. Don't have to lay a hand on the kid."

"No, really. Dad already let him have it, and I want to face my own problems."

"Okay, but my offer still stands."

"I'll keep that in mind."

They stepped inside the classroom just as the final bell sounded. Mr. Archer raised an eyebrow at them then told the class to open to page two-fifty-three. She and Braylon scrambled to the nearest empty seats.

Halfway through the class, her phone vibrated. Again and again. Someone was texting her repeatedly. And she couldn't check it. If she so much as pulled it out, the teacher could take it away, and she wouldn't get it back until after school. Maybe not even then. Mr. Archer was known for keeping them until a parent showed up for it.

The buzzing drove her crazy, and it was all she could do to act like everything was normal. She couldn't focus on anything else.

Finally, she couldn't take it any longer. She raised her hand.

Mr. Archer threw her an exasperated look. "Yes, Miss Fleshman?"

"I need to see the nurse."

He tilted his head. "Why?"

So much for keeping her ugly arm hidden. She pulled down her sleeve. Her phone vibrated yet again. "I think one of these cuts is infected. It hurts really bad."

His expression pinched. "It doesn't *look* infected."

She bit back a sarcastic comeback. "Well, do you want to take that chance? I don't think my dad, the police captain, would be too happy to hear you kept me from needed medical attention."

Mr. Archer's mouth formed a straight line. Some kids snickered.

"Fine. But I'm going to check with the nurse's office. If your arm isn't infected, we're going to have a talk during detention."

"Great." Ava gathered her things. She was pretty sure that

privacy laws meant the nurse couldn't tell the teacher anything. "Thanks."

"Your homework is still due tomorrow, start of class. Same as everyone else."

"Okay." She met Braylon's gaze before rushing out of the classroom. Before reaching the nurse's office, she stopped in the closest bathroom and went into a stall. At least she could check the texts there.

Her mouth dropped open. Forty-two new texts, and a new one came in as she stared at the screen. They were all, unsurprisingly, from Mason. She started deleting them without reading them. More came in as she worked.

Finally, Ava couldn't take it anymore. She responded.

Ava: Stop!!!

Mason: Finally a response!

Ava: Leave me alone!!

Mason: After u meet me.

Ava: Never.

Mason: Then ill keep txting.

Ava: I'll block u.

Mason: Ill find u.

Ava: U want 2 end up in jail?

Mason: I won't.

Ava took a deep breath. She'd promised Dad she wouldn't engage, but what was she supposed to do when he wouldn't stop?

Mason: Still there?

Ava: Go. Away.

Mason: Cant. Already here.

Blood drained from her head.

Ava: Where?

Mason: Near ur school.

Ava: Liar.

Mason: Nope.

She stared at the screen.

Mason: Ur wearing a blue shirt & black pants.

The phone fell from her grasp. She struggled to catch it before it hit the nasty floor.

Mason: Now do i have ur attention?

She struggled to breathe. He'd watched her walk from the bus to the school doors? Or worse, had he seen her at home? Did the psychopath know where she lived?

Mason: Dont ignore me.

Her heart raced, and she struggled to hold the phone.

Ava: What do u want?

Mason: Just 2 talk.

Ava: Yeah right.

Mason: Im ur brother. Whats the problem?

Ava: U really have 2 ask?

Mason: Im not gonna kiss u again. Not now.

Ava: Right. Cuz im not going 2 meet u.

Mason: But I came all this way.

Ava: U shouldn't have. Go c mom.

Mason: I will, but first cu.

Ava: U do realize my dads a cop?

Mason: But Parkers dad isnt.

Ava: Yes he is. Ur stupid.

Mason: No. His dad is in jail. Ur the stupid 1.

Ava's mind spun. Was he saying Dave was also Parker's dad? That wasn't possible. Mason was older. Born before Mom and Dad married, when Mom was with Dave.

Mason: Still dont believe me?

Ava: Ur wrong.

Mason: Nope.

Ava: Leave me alone. I have 2 go 2 class.

Mason: Meet me after skool.

Ava: No.

Mason: Hanna's wearing a purple dress.

Ava: Are u threatening her??

Mason: Not if u meet me.

Ava's blood boiled. What was she supposed to do? Mason could really hurt her little sister. And what if he was right about Parker? Would he tell Dad? Dad would be heartbroken.

Mason: Hello???

Whatever Ava ended up doing, she would have to delete all of these texts. Maybe keeping the ones where he said he knew what she and Hanna were wearing. That was good proof of him threatening her. No way she was going to let Dad or her brother see the ones he said about Parker.

Mason: Hanna's playing tetherball right now.

Ava: Fine. I'll meet u.

He sent a string of smirking emojis.

Mason: Good. Look 4 a txt l8r.

She didn't respond. He didn't, either. Why would he? After taking a minute to calm herself, she stuffed her phone at the bottom of her bag before leaving the bathroom.

Mr. Archer stood outside, tapping his foot and crossing his arms. "Have a nice time at the nurse's office?"

Ava stood taller. "That's where I'm going right now."

"What were you doing in the bathroom?"

"What do you think?"

"Don't get snarky with me."

She held back an eye roll. "I had to pee. Now I need the nurse to look at my arm."

"What happened to your arm?"

Ava groaned. "My brother shoved me."

"Into a cheese grater?"

"Cement."

"Why were you in the bathroom so long?"

"I don't think this is an appropriate conversation, Mr. Archer."

"What are you hiding?"

"Nothing!"

His scowl told her he didn't believe her.

"I need the nurse to look at my arm."

"Okay, but you have detention after school."

She stared at him. "For what?"

"Because I said so. Don't be late." He walked away.

Ava rubbed her temples. How was she supposed to secretly meet Mason and be in detention at the same time?

CHANGES

J ess finished her second cup of coffee, not that it helped—not with as little sleep as she got the night before.

In the next room, Sammy wailed.

"I've got him!" Willow called.

Jess closed her eyes. "Good girl! Thanks!"

After the last week she'd had, it was tempting to think life would be easier with a guy. Someone to help with everything. But she knew better. Men really don't help, don't get involved. A man would rather sit behind his phone and let the woman do all the work—helping the kids, housework, anything. Her dad, her mom's boyfriends, and Jess's ex-boyfriends all proved that point time and time again.

No. She was definitely better off without a man. Who needed that kind of stress? At least the way things were, she didn't have anyone criticizing how she took care of the kids or house. Not only that, but she had one less person to clean up after. As hard as things were now, the bright side was that she didn't have to worry about any of that.

Men. Who needed them? Not Jess.

She poured herself some more coffee, took a few sips, then went to check on the kids.

Sammy sat on Willow's lap, his face tear-stained. Daisy was nowhere to be seen.

"What happened?"

Willow rubbed Sammy's hair. "He and Daisy crashed into each other, and then he fell over and started crying. She ran off, thinking she did something wrong."

Definitely didn't need the critical voice of a man around here.

Jess reached for Sammy, who eagerly went to her arms. "You okay?"

He just sniffled.

"Can you check on your sister?"

Willow got up and left the room without a word.

Jess snuggled Sammy. "Did you hit your head?"

He shook his head no.

"Did you hurt anything?"

Sammy held out his left hand. The little finger was swollen and red.

Her heart raced. The last thing they needed was a trip to see a doctor. It was for the same reason she couldn't put them in daycare or school. No legal documentation. They also didn't have health insurance, but that would've been pointless. The kids couldn't see a doctor. Not without raising questions.

Connor came to mind, but she shoved him from her thoughts. She couldn't think about him now. It was too much, especially with all the hate comments she was getting online.

Jess looked at the finger and asked Sammy a few more questions about it. Didn't seem to be broken. Probably just landed on it funny. No need for a doctor. Or a husband. Especially not a husband. If she had one, he'd probably be yelling at her right now for allowing a kid to get hurt. Men were about blaming, not trying to make things better.

Willow came back. "She won't leave the bedroom. Says you're mad at her."

Jess took a deep breath. "I'll talk with her."

"I can hold Sammy."

Sammy clung to Jess.

Jess readjusted him. "It's okay. I'll hold him. You can keep watching your show."

Willow shrugged then plopped on the sofa.

"It's not that he doesn't *want* you," Jess reassured her. "He's just hurt and wants his mom. That's all."

"It's fine." Willow aimed the remote at the TV and pressed a button, changing the channel.

Jess went to the girls' bedroom to speak with Daisy. By the time she was done, all three kids were smiling. She finished her coffee and watched them sitting together with pride. She chastised herself for allowing the thought about needing a man. Who was she kidding? She didn't even need one to get these kids. Really, this was the ideal situation.

Minus the online drama. That she could really do without.

She set her empty mug on the side table. "Who wants to go to the new arcade?"

The girls both turned her way, eyes wide with excitement.

"Really?" Daisy asked.

"You're going to let us?" Willow covered her mouth. She'd been wanting to go more than the others.

Jess nodded. "I think today is the perfect day for it." And besides, it was a fairly long drive to get there, so if anyone recognized it once she posted pictures in her blog, they wouldn't be able to figure out where they lived. She would have to make it more of a habit, going places that were an hour or more out. Maybe even have some overnight getaways. The kids loved staying in hotels.

The social media circus would settle down before too long. It was only a matter of waiting it out. People would get bored and move on when the next big piece of drama hit. Something new always came about. It might take a few weeks, but people *would* forget about her.

Hopefully that Alexander guy would give up. He kind of worried her. There was something about him that struck her as different from the typical Internet hater.

She shoved him from her mind and started packing for the outing. All she needed to do was show people there was nothing to worry about. That everyone was getting up in arms about nothing. Just a single mom who liked to blog about her kids. What was wrong with that?

The kids ran around, packing snacks and other necessities for an outing. Jess grabbed a baseball cap and stuck it on her head. Then a thought struck her. People would be on the lookout for her kids, thanks to all the online drama.

"Hey, let's cut our hair before going out. Willow, did you still want to color your hair?"

Her eyes lit up. "Are you going to let me?"

"Yeah, I was just waiting for the right time. Today has that feel, don't you think?"

Willow stared at her in disbelief. "Really?"

"Let's do this. I ordered the color weeks ago."

"I can have a pixie cut?" Daisy asked.

Jess hated to chop her long hair, but drastic times called for drastic measures. "Sure. I found some videos online I can follow."

"Yippee!"

Sammy rubbed his eyes.

Jess picked him up. "I'm going to lay him down for a nap, then we'll set up our own personal hair salon."

The girls squealed.

Jess's stomach knotted. Hopefully the hair changes would be enough. If the haters didn't ease up as quickly as she expected, she'd really have to start getting creative.

UNBENDING

va sat under a fire extinguisher in a hallway kids never went down. She needed to text Mason with privacy.

Before she could even start her message, Braylon sent her a message.

Braylon: Where ru?

Ava: Running l8

Braylon: Want me 2 grab ur lunch?

Ava: Sure. Cu soon.

She added some heart emoticons for good measure before turning back to the conversation with her irritating and pushy half-brother.

Ava: We're gonna have 2 meet l8r.

Mason: Nope.

Ava: I have detention b/c of u!

Mason: Not my fault.

Her blood boiled. She was probably going to end up punching his ugly face after school. It was inevitable.

Ava: Is 2. U wouldn't stop txting me.

Mason: Not my concern.

Ava: If u want 2 stay off my dad's radar it is.

Mason: I don't care abt him.

Ava: Cop, remember??

Mason: Look at Hanna playin' tag. She's so happy. H8 2 spoil the fun.

Yep. She was definitely going to punch him. All the way into next week if possible.

Mason: Still there?

Ava: I can't get out of detention! Thx 4 that btw.

Mason: Find a way. Im watching her.

Ava: Fine! Somewhere public.

Mason: Nope.

Ava: Yes. Or I'm telling my dad everything.

Mason: U wouldn't dare.

Ava: Want 2 try me?

Mason: U better chill b4 we meet.

Ava: Public place.

Mason: That coffee shop by ur skool.

Ava: Fine.

Mason: Dont b l8.

She didn't bother responding to that one. He'd want the last word, anyway.

Braylon sent her another text, wanting to know where she was.

Ava sent him a quick text, then rushed to the cafeteria and scarfed down some tasteless school food before it was time for her next class.

The rest of the day went by in a blur as her mind constantly went back to Mason. She was going to have to delete all those messages before her dad saw them. Not only that, but she'd have to keep her meeting secret and explain not only why she had detention but why she'd skipped it.

Dad was *so* going to ground her. But what other choice did Mason leave her? Ava couldn't risk him doing anything to Hanna. She was only nine—still a baby in so many ways.

Maybe Ava's determination to protect her sister would win her points with Dad. But not the fact that he wanted her to stop texting Mason.

What if she actually got her dad involved? Fessed up to everything that was going on and let him show up at the coffee shop? Then at least she wouldn't get in trouble for missing detention. She'd still have it, but she wouldn't dig herself deeper into trouble.

But Hanna... If Mason saw their dad show up, he might be able to slip away and get to Hanna first. Make Ava pay for not doing what he wanted.

No. She needed to handle this herself. It was her fault for not blocking his number in the first place. Now he was threatening Hanna, and he was crazy enough to follow through. She couldn't risk pissing him off and sending him to her little sister.

Ava would never forgive herself if that happened.

"Earth to Ava."

She turned to Braylon and slammed her locker shut. "Yeah?"

"What's going on? You've been in your own world all day."

"Tired, I guess. My arm hurts."

"That's all?"

Ava shrugged.

He held her gaze. "I feel like you're shutting me out."

"I'm not."

"There isn't anything you're keeping from me?"

She looked away. "We're not married. I don't have to tell you everything."

"So, you are keeping something from me?"

"I didn't say that."

"You didn't have to."

She sighed. "Family stuff is really complicated right now. That's all."

"Because of the engagement? Your brother acting out?"

Ava chewed on her lower lip. "Something like that."

"What aren't you telling me?"

129

She glanced at a clock. "Warning bell's about to go off. I need to go."

"Ava." He gave her puppy-dog eyes, which made her stomach flip-flop. "You know I'm only asking because I care, right?"

"I'll text you after school." She rushed past him.

He grabbed her shoulder. "Wait. This isn't about Mason, is it?"

Her stomach tightened. "I can't be late for class. I already have detention."

"*Is* it Mason?"

She didn't look at him. "I have to go." Then she raced away, forcing herself into the middle of a crowd, ensuring he wouldn't be able to follow her. And it worked. She made it to her classroom just as the final bell rang, and Braylon wasn't in sight.

By the time her last class ended, her stomach was tied in more knots than the necklace she'd recently lent to Hanna. Speaking of Hanna, Ava needed to get to the coffee shop before Mason thought she'd skipped out on him and he headed back to the elementary school.

She headed for the back of the school as most kids flooded for the front to load onto buses or go to their sport practices.

"Ava!" called a male voice behind her.

She hesitated. But only for a moment. There was no time to lose. No time to even look back and see if it was Mr. Archer or Braylon, or someone else completely.

Ava burst into a run. Footsteps thundered behind her. She ran faster, her heart threatening to explode from her chest. Nobody was going to keep her from that coffee shop. She'd let Mason kidnap her if it meant keeping Hanna safe. Ava knew how to get out of being held captive. She actually liked the thought of having the chance to beat the crap out of her half-brother.

The footsteps behind her grew closer. She was almost to the door. Then she only had to get across an open soccer field before she reached the road. Once there, she would be halfway to the coffee shop.

Just as her palms made contact with the metal bar to open the door, fingers brushed her arms.

"Fire!" That was what her dad had taught her to scream if she was ever in trouble. People would run to help put out a fire. Not so much if someone was in other kinds of danger.

"Ava!" It was Braylon.

She threw her weight against the door and stumbled into the bright sunlight.

"Ava!"

"Don't try to stop me!"

"I already have."

She spun around and stared at her boyfriend. "What?"

"Earlier, I saw your phone had an alert. A message from Mason. I put two and two together. You're planning to meet him, aren't you?"

Her mouth dropped open. "You don't know what's at stake! I have to go!"

Braylon shook his head. "Don't make matters worse than they already are. Let's get to detention before you end up with more."

She stepped away from him. "I don't have a choice."

"He's not at the coffee shop."

Blood drained from her face. "Hanna!"

"He's not there, either. Come on."

"What's going on?" Ava demanded.

"I'll tell you on the way." He glanced at the time. "If we hurry, you won't be late."

"Where is he if he's not at the coffee shop?"

"Come on."

"Tell me!" Acid churned in her gut. "I have to protect my sister!"

He took a deep breath. "Jail."

She gave him a double-take. "What?"

"Come *on*." He laced his fingers through hers and led her down the hallway.

"What do you mean, he's in *jail*? How do you know?"

"Because I told your dad, Ava."

She skidded to a stop and stared at him in disbelief. "You what?"

"What else was I supposed to do? You were supposed to stop texting him, but you didn't. He's dangerous."

Her mind raced too fast to form words. All she knew was that her dad was going to be furious. Maybe *she'd* be the one going to military school instead of Parker.

Braylon nodded. "Come on. You need to get to detention before—"

"Before I'm late. I know." She stormed ahead of him. How could Braylon turn on her like that? He hadn't even asked her about the text. Just assumed he knew what was going on. Then he went to her dad? Unbelievable!

"Ava!"

"Go away."

"You don't have to face him. He's not going to hurt your sister. I did the right thing, and you know it."

She stopped and turned around.

He crashed into her.

"You did *not* do the right thing! Do you hear me? You went behind my back!"

"Like you didn't go behind my back?"

"I wasn't hiding anything that had anything to do with you!" She clenched her fists.

"Putting yourself in harm's way doesn't affect me? Are you serious?"

"Yes!"

He shook his head and drew in a deep breath. His mouth formed a straight line and his nostrils flared. "Guess we'll have to agree to disagree."

"That's where you're wrong."

Braylon looked at the time. "You have one minute to get there, and it's across the building."

"I kind of don't care."

"Why are you so determined to make everything worse for yourself?"

Heart pounding, she narrowed her eyes at him. "Do you know what's the worst part about all of this?"

He raked his fingers through his hair. "What?"

"I thought I could trust you." She spun around and marched toward the detention room.

By the time she got there, she was four minutes late.

The teacher glanced up at her. "Name?"

"Ava Fleshman."

He scanned a paper on a clipboard. "You're not on the list. Sure you have detention today?"

She gave him a double-take, trying to figure out what happened. Mr. Archer had definitely given her detention.

"I guess not." Ava spun around and trudged away.

Braylon stood behind her, his arms crossed. "Now we can talk."

"Not a chance." She raced away so she could get to the elementary school and make sure her sister was safe.

GUILT

A lex flung the covers off and sat up. He'd been tossing and turning, unable to get any decent sleep. He kept dreaming about the accident. The deceased driver.

It could've so easily been him years earlier. He'd raced that road countless times. Granted, he'd never once tried to maneuver that curve at high speeds. But that didn't change the fact that he'd still stupidly put his life on the line. Not only his life, but others. More often than not, he'd had someone with him.

Why was he lucky enough to survive? Because he was just a little less stupid than the two drivers the night before? Was that the only thing standing between leaving Ariana fatherless and not?

He lay back down and closed his eyes. It was pointless. His mind wouldn't stop racing.

Maybe reading would help. He grabbed his phone and checked social media.

Everyone was talking about the mommy blogger's newest post. His thumb hovered over the link. If he started reading that, he would get himself worked up. He would be certain to lose more sleep. But he needed to know what she posted now.

Had she finally spoken the truth about Connor? Admitted there was no custody battle?

It was doubtful. His money was on her posting business as usual. Probably something about the kids, with no mention of her missing son again.

Alex pressed the link and scrolled through the post. It took a minute to load because of all the pictures. They were of the kids at an arcade, but that wasn't what caught his attention.

Each of the children's appearance had been altered dramatically. The oldest had darker hair. The middle one had much shorter hair—so short it almost looked like a boy's cut. And the toddler's curls had been trimmed.

Did she really think that would be enough to keep her from being found? Now that she'd posted those photos, everyone knew what the kids' new look was. She still didn't post any with her in them. Not even a belly shot this time.

The thought of her reproducing again sent a shiver through him.

He wanted to punch the screen. Where was Connor? When would the truth finally come out? Somebody had to know something. Or could at least figure it out based on her posts. The truth had to be in there, maybe buried, definitely hidden, but in there. Alex was familiar enough with human psychology to know people never fully hid the truth.

There were ways to figure out what was going on, especially with all the technology available. It used to be easy enough to get away with murder—nobody saw them do it? Great. There was no evidence. But now cold cases were being solved every day thanks to the constantly-improving technologies taking trace evidence and pointing to the killers.

It was a great time to be an officer. Even so, there were frustrating cases like this. The mommy blogger was all over the web, but still nobody had a clue where she actually was. What happened to the little boy?

Maybe it was time for yet another email. Alex could take a different approach. Appeal to her common sense. Tell her that if she would simply provide some proof that the boy was actually with his father, people would leave her alone. They'd be satisfied.

Obviously, Alex didn't believe that was possible, but on the slim chance that she was telling the truth, she could stop wasting everyone's time. If not, hopefully that kind of a letter—one that sounded like he wanted to help, like he might believe her—would encourage her to come out with the truth.

Clearly, one email wouldn't push her to confess to everything, but with any luck, it would be a start. Get her moving in that direction.

Either that, or it would send her further from the truth. Make her more defensive. She'd already changed the kids' appearances. Told stories with no credibility whatsoever. Blocked more people.

Alex had plenty of email addresses. He'd collected them over the years in various stages of life. He was pretty sure he could still get into his first one. One he'd made when he was learning to type and only emailed his grandparents.

The mommy blogger could keep blocking him, but he would just write from different addresses. Easy. He'd wear her down. Ask questions to draw out answers she didn't intend to reveal.

He went over to his email and used voice dictation to quickly get the message written. It took some editing to get it right because some things always got messed up. He was tempted to leave the mention of her being a mommy hogger, but he fixed it.

Once he was sure it was as close to perfect as he could get it, he pressed send.

Then his exhaustion hit. He'd spent most of his allotted sleep time tossing and turning. Now with—he checked the time—two hours left, his eyelids were growing heavy. He would either be next to useless on the job or he would have to sleep later and skip family time. Neither option was one he wanted, but he *had* spent some time with Zoey and the twins before going to bed.

He changed the time on his alarm and closed his eyes, sleep overtaking him. With any luck, he'd have a reply to his email when he woke.

STRESS

Nick tapped his steering wheel as he looked at the house. Ava and Parker were supposed to be inside, but given all the trouble they'd been throwing his way, it was anyone's guess where they actually were. Maybe he needed to have them go to his parents' house after school like Hanna.

"Are we going in?" Hanna asked from the backseat.

He took a deep breath. "Yeah. Sorry, kiddo. Just thinking."

"About the wedding?"

If only life were that simple. "Are you excited for it?"

"I can't wait! Genevieve said I can pick out the fanciest dress I want."

Nick smiled and patted her hand. "And I'm sure you'll look like a princess."

"Dad, I'm too old for princesses."

"You are?"

"I'm *nine.*"

"Genevieve still likes princesses. She said she dressed as one for Halloween a few years ago."

Hanna tilted her head and gave him a quizzical expression. "Really?"

"That's what she told me."

"Hmm. Maybe I wouldn't mind looking like a princess."

Nick smiled. At least one of his kids still enjoyed the simple things in life. "Good. Because I'm sure you'll look like one."

"Just don't tell Ella that I'm trying to be a princess."

He nodded knowingly. "Is Ella why you didn't want to be a princess?"

Hanna shrugged.

Nick squeezed her hand. "Don't let your friends dictate what you like or don't like. You're *you*, and there's nothing wrong with anything you like."

She frowned. "I don't want to be a baby."

"You aren't. You know, I played with toys when my friends all said it was uncool."

"You did?"

"Sure did. My favorites were my wrestling action figures. I loved setting up wrestling matches and determining who got to win."

"Wrestling action figures?"

"They were really popular."

"Weird."

Nick chuckled. "I might still have them somewhere. Grandma tried to throw them out a few times, but I always managed to save them."

"I want to see them!"

Glad for the reprieve from the stress, short lived as it probably would be, he agreed to look for them, then they headed inside. The house was empty, not that it surprised Nick. Ava was probably worried about getting in trouble for texting Mason after agreeing not to and Parker was more than likely down the street with his friends. One of the moms made snacks for all the boys daily and let them play football after doing an hour of homework.

Nick found the storage box filled with action figures and brought it out for Hanna.

Her eyes widened. "They're like Barbies!"

"They're *nothing* like dolls."

"Boys can play with dolls, Dad. It's fine."

"I never said it wasn't. I just said *these ones* aren't dolls. They—"

"Pink pants?" She reached for one. "Cool!"

"It was a popular color for guys back then." Nick sat, pulled out a few more action figures, then told her about his favorites and some of their best moves. They play-wrestled for a little while before Nick had to text the older kids to come home for dinner.

"Can I help?" Hanna jumped up. "I feel like making tacos."

"You do?"

"Yeah. Can we have them?"

"Let me see if we have shells."

"I'll check!" Hanna skipped out of the room.

Nick sighed. If only kids could stay that age forever. He checked his phone. Parker had replied, saying he'd be a few minutes. Nothing from Ava. He sent her another text.

"We have shells!" Hanna called. "The organic purple ones. Can I start the meat?"

He started to tell her to wait, but she was a pro at using the stove. Even she was growing up. "Go for it!"

"Yay! Thanks, Dad!"

He called Ava, since she wasn't replying to the texts. They weren't even marked as read, but she should've seen them in her notifications.

Voicemail.

Nick grumbled under his breath, then sent one last text telling her she would lose her cell phone if she ignored him.

That got a response.

Ava: I'll b on my way. Arguing w/ Braylon.

Nick: Give him a break. He cares about you.

Ava: Cu in a few.

Before he could respond, Genevieve called. He accepted the call rather than trying to have the last word with his daughter.

"Hi, beautiful."

"Hey, handsome." He could hear the smile in her voice. "Just calling to see how everything's going with Ava and Parker."

"Could be worse." They'd both seen a lot worse on the job.

"That's not what I asked. Are you okay? You sound tired."

"It's that obvious?" He rubbed his temple.

"To be fair, I do know you better than most."

"I'm glad for that." Nick filled her in on the latest without going into too many details.

"You arrested Mason?"

"Personally. That kid really is a punk."

"I believe it. Is there enough to hold him? Stalking laws still aren't the best."

Nick sighed. "No, they're not. But between some stuff on his record back East and what was found on his phone, we have enough to keep him. Assuming somebody isn't crazy enough to post his bail."

"You think his grandparents would?"

"Or the girlfriend who traveled across the country with him. If they have enough cash between them." The aroma of taco seasoning drifted down the hall into the room. "I'd better check on Hanna. She's making dinner. Do you and Tinsley want to come over?"

"I'd love to, but Tinsley's in with her therapist right now."

"You're still welcome to come over."

"We'd love to, but I'll have to see if she's up to it. Sometimes these sessions really drain her. Depends on what they end up talking about. The majority of her life is a sore subject."

"I'm sure it is." Nick felt bad for the girl who'd grown up with cop killers for parents and used her for bait to abduct and torture officers and cadets.

They said their goodbyes, then he checked on Hanna, who had the kitchen filled with taco ingredients. Meat sizzled in a pan, cut vegetables sat on plates, and she was shredding cheese.

"It's almost ready." She beamed.

"I can't believe you did all of that on your own."

"Maybe I'll be a chef at a fancy restaurant one day."

"Then I'll eat there every night."

The front door burst open and Parker dumped his football gear on the floor. "My team won again!"

"Ever think about trying out for the school team?"

He shook his head. "I just like playing for fun with my friends. Not with the stuck-up jocks at school."

"You might enjoy it."

"Maybe." Parker kicked off his shoes.

"Wash up. It's almost ready."

He headed down the hall without a word.

Nick was about to text Ava again, when she walked through the door. She looked at him, then looked away quickly.

"Did you work things out with Braylon?"

She glared at him.

"Did you notice you got out of detention?"

Her face paled. "You know about that?"

"I'm the one who got you out of it."

"What?"

"Let's just say I had a chat with the teacher. He shouldn't give you any more problems when you need to see the nurse."

"How did you—?"

"Don't worry about it. Let's just focus on moving on."

She glanced over at her sister. "The only reason I agreed to meeting him was because he threatened her."

"I know." Nick nodded.

"Do you know everything?"

"I like to think so." The corners of his mouth twitched.

She didn't look nearly as amused. "Did he tell you everything?"

"Phone records. Nothing is as private as it feels when it comes to technology. Go wash up. Your sister made tacos."

"They're ready!" Hanna announced.

Parker came back out, now wearing joggers and a hoodie. He glared at Ava, who returned the favor.

Nick held back a groan. "You two better start getting along before I have to call a family meeting."

The kids exchanged an annoyed glance. They knew what that meant—a really long talk about feelings, and that everyone would have to own up to their actions.

"We're fine," Ava said.

"Yeah." Parker put a stiff arm around her shoulder. "Perfectly fine."

Nick knew it wouldn't be that easy, but hoped it was at least a start.

PLOTTING

J ess pressed her back against the heat pad, holding it between her and the chair. Taking the kids to the arcade and the long drive, both ways, had more than done her in. And now at least, she could once again enjoy the comments on her new post. Blocking the haters had been the right decision.

Not that there weren't still a few that slipped through, but she blocked those as they came. It was easy enough. She could keep a handle on it. It was the social media insanity that was making her stomach churn acid. She could block people, but not get rid of the posts or the hashtag—which was still trending, though not as high as before. Hopefully, it would drop off completely soon.

She just needed to keep convincing people everything was fine. And she was sure to post lots of pictures of the kids smiling wide this time. She's snapped pictures that captured them having the time of their lives.

Nobody could argue with that. The kids were fine. They weren't emotionally damaged because of Connor moving away. They'd moved on because she was a good mom. Their happy grins proved that much.

Jess replied to a few comments then checked her email before heading to bed.

A new email from Alexander. She really needed to block him from sending her emails. Out of curiosity, she opened it first.

And immediately regretted that decision.

It was long, for starters. The wall of text made her already-growing headache throb. Didn't he know that white space was a writer's friend? But ironically, the length piqued her interest. She pressed her back harder against the heating pad and read the message.

He still didn't believe anything she said about Connor. Claimed that the truth would come out one way or another. Said it always did. Like he was some kind of telepath.

Jess was tempted to delete and block before finishing, but something urged her to read it through. She wouldn't give him the satisfaction of replying, but he'd never know she took in every word he wrote.

As soon as she finished it, she noticed something. His email signature. It linked to a blog.

He was a blogger, too?

She let the pointer hover over the link for a moment before clicking.

Jess's stomach dropped to the floor when she saw the header. He wrote exclusively about missing and exploited children. And a quick perusal of the site showed it was popular. Not as well-ranked as hers, of course, but the man knew what he was doing. And from the looks of it, he had been doing it for a while.

That explained why he was so adamant. Why he claimed to know so much about everything. And most importantly, that he was serious about not dropping the subject.

Which was fine. There was no way he could prove anything, one way or the other. She could block him, then she wouldn't have to think about him. She was about to click away from his site, when a recent post title caught her attention.

It had the annoying hashtag. Had he been the one to start it?

Anger stormed in her chest. She clicked to the post, as much as she hated to give him another page view, and read it over.

He *had* been the one to start it. #MommyBloggerMayhem had been his stupid idea, and worse, it had taken off. *Still* trending, even though there were real problems in the world beyond a single mom trying to raise her kids.

It was time to shut him up for good. Fury pulsated through her veins. Her fingers shook as she hastily typed a response to his email. She told him in no uncertain terms how wrong he was and that he needed to put a stop to the insanity, that he needed to stop harassing a hurting single mom who had just lost custody of one of her beautiful children.

Then she hesitated. Would that be enough, or did she need to take it a step further and threaten the superiority right out of him?

Stupid men. She could definitely do without a single one of them. If only womankind could carry on without them.

That settled it. He needed to be put in his place.

She *would* threaten him. Where it hurt. He'd mentioned being a dad. She'd see how he liked having people say things about *his* kids.

Her fingers could barely keep up with her mind as she typed the message. She could hardly think straight as she read over what she'd written and fixed it until it was as close to perfect as she could get it.

Once he read that, he'd leave her alone. If he cared about his kids, anyway. *She* would drop a subject if someone threatened to do the things she's just written out.

Then she could finally get back to blogging in peace. All she wanted was to be able to have a good time with her kids. Go places, blog about their adventures, and just enjoy being a mom.

Was that really so much to ask for? Seemed pretty simple.

Pressure built around her temples and near the back of her

neck. Time to get some sleep before the kids woke, which was usually pretty early.

She'd wanted to look for her next baby. That would have to wait until the next day. Besides, with Alexander out of the way, she would have plenty of time for that.

She pressed send. Freedom was hers again.

THREAT

Alex sipped his coffee as he went over paperwork. After dealing with the racing accident, he was more than happy to be at his desk. He'd only had to go out on two calls this shift, and they'd both been minor issues—at least compared to a fatality involving a teenager. Not much older than Ariana.

He closed his eyes and shoved the thought from his head. His daughter had a good head on her shoulders. She made good choices. Good grades and winning awards were her goals. She was thinking about student government.

"You okay?"

Alex glanced up to see Detective Sanchez, concern in her eyes. He nodded. "Paperwork. It's tedious."

Sanchez leaned against Alex's desk. "I mean, how are you doing after pulling the DB out of the car?"

Alex's stomach clenched at the mention of the body. "All in a day's work."

"Yeah, but that stuff can be hard to deal with. It doesn't get easier, you know. Not for those of us who care and don't get calloused. Was that your first DB?"

He shook his head no. "Remember that holdup at the convenience over on Nineteenth and Hollow Drive? Or that drug deal gone bad by the train tracks a couple of months ago?"

"Those guys were attempting to murder others. It's not quite the same as a young kid with his whole life in front of him. This was senseless and preventable."

"What are you getting at, Detective?"

She gave him a sympathetic smile. "I'm sure you've heard this before, but you can set up an appointment with the precinct's therapist any time. There isn't any shame in needing to talk things through. In fact, sometimes it's required."

"Are you saying I need to make an appointment?"

"No. Just throwing it out there. Something to think about."

"Okay. Thanks. My sister's a counselor, too. I could talk with her if I felt the need. She's helped my wife through some things."

"Good. Well, I'll see you tomorrow. I'm heading out a few minutes early today."

Alex glanced at the time. "Shift's already almost over?"

"Time flies when you're having fun." Sanchez nodded toward his paperwork.

"Right." They said their goodbyes, then he started filing everything away.

Wilson walked by and tapped Alex's desk. "Check your email. There's an update with the Potter case."

"Is it urgent?"

"Just have a look." Wilson walked away.

Alex held back a groan. After hardly getting any sleep the day before, he was more eager than usual to get home. Whatever the email said, he would deal with it the next day. He typed in the password to his laptop then opened his email, found the message, and read it over. The suspect had been arrested two towns over on unrelated charges. Definitely something he could deal with the next day. He shut down the computer and picked up his cell phone, ready to clock out.

An alert on the screen showed an email from the mommy blogger.

He blinked a few times, hardly able to believe his eyes. She'd responded? He tapped the notification and unlocked the screen with his thumbprint, his pulse drumming in his ears.

ALEXANDER,

You need to stop your smear campaign. Clearly, you have something to prove. That much is clear by your blog. Find a new hobby that doesn't involve attacking a single mom who just lost custody of a child. How low can you get, really? Pathetic, that's what you are. Worse, actually.

Get a life and focus on kids who are actually in danger. No, I'm not happy about Connor living with his dad now. It breaks my heart, but there's no reason to start a whole hashtag movement and rile up all of the Internet against me. Seriously, who picks on a single mom of four? Someone lower than a worm, that's who.

Leave me and my kids alone or you're going to regret it. Just stick with your blog and actual endangered children. My kids are all safe, loved, and happy. All of them! Do you hear me?

If I ever hear from you again or see you mentioning me online, you will regret it. But I won't go to you. I'll find a way to your kids. You have three, right? One's in school, isn't she? Guess what? Things happen at school, or on the way to and from. Wouldn't want something to go wrong, would you?

Are we on the same page? In case I haven't made myself crystal clear —stop your campaign against me or your kids will pay. And don't think this is a way you can draw me out. I won't do it myself. You'll never find me. Ever.

~A LOVING mother

ALEX SHOOK as he read the message several times. If she was trying to convince him that she was dangerous and crazy, then she'd succeeded. Threatening his kids while at the same time trying to convince him that she was a loving mom?

The woman was certifiable.

And now Alex might have enough to convince Nick to put police resources on her.

He took screenshots of the message before going over to her blog to see if she had posted it there. There was a new post, but it didn't mention him.

Connor was in some of the pictures.

Alex's breath hitched. The missing child was there? He read the post, which explained that he'd come to their home for a quick visitation. The mom lamented that her ex wanted nothing to do with his other kids and that he hated being forced to drop Connor off for a few hours. She talked about what a great time the kids all had together, and that the boy was happy and healthy with his dad, though he'd begged to move home. She claimed he'd clung to her when the dad arrived to take him back.

Something about the post didn't sit right with him. He re-read the post and studied the pictures. The kids were all smiling and happy. Almost too happy. Like she'd gone to serious effort to make everyone think all was well.

Then it struck him. Why hadn't he noticed it before?

While all the pictures were inside her house—as many were in other posts—the kids were wearing different outfits in almost every picture. Their hair lengths were all varied. Connor had a scratch on his arm in a couple, but not the rest. None of them had the children's new hairstyles.

These were all old photos.

She'd staged Connor's visitation.

It was a complete farce.

This *had* to be enough to convince Nick. They needed the station's resources to get to the bottom of this.

Alex looked at the time. The captain should be in his office. He gathered his things, clocked out, then knocked on Nick's door.

Nick waved Alex in. "Morning. How are you doing? I heard you were on the scene at the wreck."

"I'm fine. That's not why I came here."

"Have a seat." Nick turned to his computer screen. "What's going on?"

Alex waited for his friend to turn to him, but he didn't. "That mommy blogger threatened my children."

Nick turned to him. "What?"

"She told me that if I didn't leave her alone, she'd hurt one of my kids."

"You're not harassing her, are you?"

Alex narrowed his eyes. "Seriously? You told me to use my blog, and that's what I did."

"I have to ask. It sounds like that's what she's accusing you of doing."

"She's lying about her missing son! I have more proof."

Nick sighed. "She's in the area?"

"Now that she's threatened my family, this falls into our jurisdiction. But yes, I still believe she's close. She took her kids to that new arcade about an hour from here. I recognize it from when I took Ari and your kids. Remember, Parker won one of the Grand Opening prizes?"

"Show me what you have." Nick rubbed his temples.

Alex first let him read the email, then he showed him the blog posts. "See? There's no way these pictures are from the same morning. The kids' hair doesn't go from short to long overnight. And a scratch doesn't heal between breakfast and snack time."

"And you're sure that arcade is the same one you took our kids to?"

"I'm certain. Show the post to any of the kids, and they'll tell you."

Nick tapped his desk and looked deep in thought. "Your evidence is more compelling this time around. I'll give you permission to use police resources for this, but you have to promise me two things."

"Anything."

"First, this can't take precedence over the cases we have now."

Alex leaned forward. "No problem."

"And second, you need to do everything by the book. Fill out all the proper paperwork, give even more detail in the report than you've given me. She's right about it potentially looking bad—an officer going after a single mom. Handle this with care, Alex."

Excitement drummed through him. "The utmost care."

Nick nodded then turned to his computer, tapping on the keys.

"Everything okay?"

"Yeah." Nick didn't look up.

"You seem kind of distracted."

"Huh?" He turned to Alex.

"I said you're distracted."

"Mason was threatening Ava, and I arrested him yesterday. I'm thinking about paying Dave a visit."

It took Alex a moment to process everything. "How long can we hold Mason?"

"Long enough. He has some charges back home, so it's complicated."

"And how do you think talking with Dave will help?"

"They've probably been in contact. I doubt Mason has been doing all of this on his own. The kid really doesn't seem that bright."

"If you do see Dave, take me with you."

"On what grounds?"

Alex clenched his fists. "You really have to ask?"

"You aren't in any way involved with Mason. That's why I would question him."

"I need to know if he suspects anything about—" Alex lowered his voice. "—the twins."

Nick shook his head. "He'd have spoken up at the trial. And it's a moot point. The man is never getting out of prison alive. He can't get custody."

"I need to know."

"Focus on the blogger. And your cases. Mostly your cases."

Alex rose. "Let me know when you go to see Dave."

The two friends stared each other down before Alex headed out, sure it would be another nearly sleepless day.

VENT

"Ava! Wait up!"

"What?" She spun around and stopped in the middle of the track, then waited for Emma to catch up.

"Where are you going?"

"I'm going to walk home."

"That's going to take hours."

Ava shrugged. "I could use the space to think."

"Why not just take the bus and have space at home?"

"What do you want, Emma?"

"We're worried about you. Braylon hates that you won't talk to him."

"He knows what he did."

"What *did* he do?"

"I don't want to talk about it. Space, remember?"

Emma frowned. "We're friends. Talk to me."

"You'll miss your bus."

"I can call for a ride later."

Ava pulled some hair behind her ear and chewed on her lower lip. It might actually be helpful to talk to Emma. Dad and Braylon were too close to the situation to hear her out.

"Let's get some ice cream. I heard that shop by the pet store is having a deal on waffle cones today. An extra scoop for free, or something like that."

Ice cream did sound good.

"My treat." Emma tilted her head.

"Okay, you win."

"Come on!" She dragged Ava across the street and down the block.

Ten minutes later, they sat on a park bench with their over-flowing waffle cones, watching little kids at the playground.

"So, why won't you talk to Braylon?"

Ava sighed. Maybe she didn't want to talk about it, after all.

"He really cares about you. Whatever he did, he didn't mean to piss you off."

"Is that what he said?" Ava finished off the scoop of mint chocolate chip.

"No. He's a guy. All he said was, you wouldn't talk to him. The rest was written all over his face."

Ava started on her scoop of cookie dough.

"Are you going to break up with him?"

"I don't know about anything right now."

Emma nearly dropped her cone, but caught it. "You're seriously thinking about dumping him?"

Ava shrugged.

"You can't! You guys are totally meant to be together. And besides, the four of us get along so well. One of the football players called us the four musketeers."

"Is that what you're worried about?"

"No. I'm just pointing it out. It's *you* I'm worried about. You got detention and you keep hiding your arm. Now you're mad at Braylon. What's the matter?"

The air felt like it was pressing in on her. Emma was probably telling the truth about being worried, but pointing everything out made everything seem worse.

"I won't tell anyone, no matter what it is. Did you meet someone else?"

"No! It's not like that. My family is royally screwed up, and it's even worse than normal lately. I didn't want Braylon to get involved, but he did. It wasn't his place."

"Was he trying to help?"

"Probably, but he did the opposite. And he didn't even ask me what I thought. He just did what he thought was best, but he doesn't know. He doesn't!"

Emma's eyes widened with each word Ava spoke. "What did he do?"

"He got someone arrested."

She covered her mouth with her free hand. "For real?"

"Do I look like I'm kidding? I mean, the guy had it coming, but he's going to get out. Then he's going to hurt people."

"Is your family part of the mafia or something?"

"My dad's the police captain. Do you really think we're in the mob?"

Emma shrugged. "It's kind of sounding like it, the way you're describing it. Is the guy who got arrested going to kill people?"

"He could."

"Really?"

"Wouldn't surprise me. Especially after being arrested. He always told me that if he went to jail because of me, I wouldn't live to regret it."

Emma dropped the cone on the ground. Pink ice cream splattered on both of them.

"Now do you see why I'm not speaking to Braylon?" Ava brushed the dessert off her pants.

"Who is this guy? Is *he* a mob boss?"

"I don't know anyone in the mafia!"

"Then who is he?"

"Just some jerk I happen to be related to. Now I have to figure out what to do when he gets out. He'll come after me now. That's for sure."

"Can't you get a restraining order to keep him away?"

"Like a piece of paper is going to keep him from me. Plus, I'm not the only one he's going to hurt. I have more to think about than just myself."

"Maybe Braylon can help."

"He's already done enough."

"But does he know that turning that dangerous guy in made things worse for you?"

Ava shook her head.

"If you tell him exactly what's going on—more than you're telling me—he can do something to make it right."

"He can't protect my family from a psychopath. Besides, I don't want him ending up next on the hit list."

Emma straightened her back. "There's an actual hit list? Like in the movies?"

"In the fact that he has plans to hurt certain people, yeah there is a list."

"But the guy's in jail, right?"

Ava nodded. "For now."

"You think he might get out?"

"People get out of jail all of the time."

"Even people like that?"

Ava frowned. "Trust me. I know what I'm talking about. Things go wrong all the time. People like him have resources. If he knows someone with money, he just has to make a call, then one way or another he'll find a way out. Lawyers, bail, who knows what else? They have ways."

"What are you going to do?"

"Keep as many people out of it as possible, which is why you can't tell anyone about this."

Emma swallowed. "You think he'd come after me?"

"If he thinks you might be dangerous."

"Me? Dangerous?"

"If he thinks you'd rat him out. You know, like Braylon did—but it looks like I'm the one who told my dad."

Emma chewed on a nail. "Is it safe for you to be at school?"

"Yeah. It's fine."

"Even though...?" Emma's voice trailed off and she looked around.

"He's in jail, right? What can he do to me?"

"But you just said he can get out."

"And if he did, my dad would let me know right away. If he gets out, then I need to worry."

Emma turned back to her. "I'm worried now."

"You're fine. He's obsessed with me." Ava felt bad being so vague, especially since Mason *could* potentially go after Emma like he'd threatened with Hanna. But even if he did that, it would only be to get Ava to do what he wanted. And she would, to protect her friends and family. It wasn't their fault. She was the one he wanted.

And she would face him. She'd been more than ready before Braylon had made things worse.

"What are you going to do about Braylon?"

Ava shrugged.

"You aren't going to break up with him, are you?"

"That's the last thing I want."

Emma met her gaze. "That's not what I asked. Are you going to break up with him?"

"I don't want to, but if it comes down to keeping him safe, then yes, I will."

"Oh, Ava." Emma took her hand.

"As long as he stays in jail, there's nothing to worry about."

Emma frowned.

Ava didn't believe it herself, either.

MEETING

Nick picked at his food, his mind miles away, his stomach twisting at the thought of eating.

Genevieve rested a hand on his leg. "Everything okay?"

He turned to her and tried to smile. "A lot on my mind."

"Understandable. Can I do anything?"

"Just don't take it personally that I'm barely eating the food you brought over."

She kissed his cheek. "Never."

He waited for the kids to finish eating, then he asked everyone to go to the living room before they scattered.

Parker groaned. "Why?"

"We're going to have a quick family meeting."

Hanna jumped from her chair. "Yay! I love family meetings."

Parker muttered something under his breath.

Nick glared at him.

He didn't apologize, but he trudged to the living room without another word.

Once everyone was settled, Nick sat next to Genevieve and looked around at each of the kids individually. "We all know that becoming a family is going to take some adjustments. There's a lot we haven't talked about, and that's why we're here now—to open the gates of communication. We won't be able to get through everything tonight, but we can at least start with whatever's on the top of your mind."

"And nothing's off limits," Genevieve added. "This is a safe place to say exactly how you feel. Respectfully, of course."

Silence hung in the air. The kids looked around everywhere except at her and Nick.

He gave it a few moments before speaking. "Really? Nobody has anything to say?"

Genevieve put her hand on his. "I can start. It can be intimidating to be the first to speak up."

Nick relaxed a little. She was definitely handling this better than he was.

She tucked her long black ponytail behind her back and took a deep breath. "I think we're all a little nervous, or maybe I'm only thinking of myself. *I'm* a little nervous."

All the kids looked at her with varying degrees of surprised expressions.

Genevieve smiled. "Today, I fought with an armed robber. Kicked the gun from his hand, struggled with him, then finally cuffed him—all while my partner was taking down another gunman. But you know what? My heart is pounding harder now than it was then. Really."

Hanna's eyes were wide. Parker and Ava looked at her with respect. Tinsley swallowed.

"As excited as we all are about the engagement," Genevieve continued, "we still have questions. Concerns. Things are going to change, and none of us knows exactly what that means. There are still a lot of unknowns—will we all move into a new house, or will Tinsley and I come here? Will you have your own room? Someone else telling you what to do? What will it be like with all of us living under one roof? Are you wondering any of these things?"

Hanna and Tinsley nodded, then so did Ava, and finally Parker.

"I have a lot of questions, too. I can only imagine that you all have plenty of your own. Change is scary, even when it's good. Even things we look forward to can cause stress and anxiety. Did you know most arguments happen around the holidays?"

"Why?" Hanna asked. "That's the best time of year."

"Because it's a change of routine. People get anxious. There are expectations and unanswered questions. It makes people edgy."

"It's true," Parker said. "Mom and Dad used to fight more around Christmas."

Ava shoved him. "Don't bring up Mom in front of Genevieve."

Nick started to say something, but Genevieve beat him to it.

"It's okay." She nodded. "I don't want any of you feeling like you can't talk about her. She's your mom, one of the most important people in your lives. I'm not threatened by that, nor am I going to try to replace her. I really believe you have enough room in your hearts for both of us, in different ways. If you want to talk about her, feel free to talk to me. I'm all ears."

"Really?" Parker studied her.

"Yes. You can ask Tinsley. Even though I've adopted her, I'm not her only mom. She has two, and that's just as it should be." Genevieve turned to Tinsley. "Are you able to talk about your parents with me? To say anything you want?"

Tinsley licked her lips and then nodded. "You just listen."

Genevieve smiled at her, then looked at the other kids. "I don't want any awkwardness or hesitation. That's not how I roll. If something's on your mind, just say it. I've been through a lot—things that would undoubtedly surprise you—and I can be very understanding. Just give me the benefit of the doubt, and I'll do the same for you. Sometimes it's hard to figure out how we feel. Let's work it out together, okay?"

Nick's heart swelled. This was going a hundred times better than he'd hoped. He'd been thinking about the meeting all day, but hadn't come up with anything half as good as what Genevieve had just said. She really was exactly what he and the kids needed. Hopefully, they could be what she and Tinsley needed.

"We can say *anything*?" Parker raised an eyebrow.

"Respectfully, yes." Genevieve nodded. "Is there something you want to say now?"

He shrugged.

"Think about it." She turned to Ava. "What about you? Any questions for me? Or anyone else?"

Ava glanced away. "I don't know."

"That's fine. If you guys want to talk to me alone, we can do that later. I'm more than happy to talk without an audience. That's a little less intimidating." She turned to Hanna. "Do you have any questions, sweetie?"

"No. I can't wait to be the flower girl!" She beamed.

"Are the rest of us going to be in the ceremony?" Ava asked.

Nick swallowed. That wasn't something he and Genevieve had had time to discuss yet.

She leaned forward. "Do you want to be?"

Ava shrugged.

"I'd be more than happy to have you and Tinsley as brides-maids, but I'll leave it up to you."

Nick looked at Parker. "And you can be one of my grooms-men. If you want to be."

The mood lightened almost immediately as everyone discussed the wedding. He didn't care much about the ceremony itself, he was just relieved the meeting had gone so well.

Then Ava glanced at her phone.

His stomach knotted. "Is someone texting you?"

Her expression tightened. "It's just Braylon."

Nick didn't respond.

"It couldn't be Mason, could it? He's in jail."

"If you *do* hear from him, you need to tell me right away. Do you understand?"

Ava's eyes narrowed, but she nodded.

Nick glanced around the living room—that Corrine had bought. Though she was in prison for life, so much of her still seeped in. Her influence was everywhere, weaving its way through everything in their lives.

He cleared his throat. "How does everyone feel about starting our new family off with a new home? One that we all pick out together?"

Parker's eyes widened. "You'd let us pick out a house?"

"Genevieve and I would have to approve, obviously. But yes, you can all have a say."

"I still want my own room," Ava said.

Nick turned to Tinsley and Hanna. "What do you two think?"

Tinsley just nodded.

Hanna leaned forward. "Can Tinsley and I share a room?"

"If she wants to."

Hanna grabbed Tinsley's hands. "Please?"

Tinsley grinned and nodded.

"Hurray!"

Nick and Genevieve exchanged a pleased glance. Things were far from perfect, but at least they were getting better.

SEARCH

Jess shoved aside toys and set her glass of wine on the coffee table before settling into the couch and finding a mindless show to stream while she got down to business. The kids had just fallen asleep, so she should have plenty of time.

Canned laughter sounded from the TV as she grabbed her laptop. Jess glanced up and chuckled at the shenanigans on the screen. She'd seen that episode enough times to know exactly what was going on even though she'd missed the punchline.

She sipped her drink as she checked her blog comments and emails. A few new haters made their way through, but she blocked them. Technology made her life so much easier. Made it possible to have her life the way it was, actually. Without the Internet, she couldn't make a living blogging. She'd have to go somewhere for work.

That thought sent a chill down her spine. It'd be much harder to raise the kids how she wanted. She'd either have to leave them home while she worked or send them to daycare or school. As it was, she didn't have to do any of that. There was no legal paperwork linking the kids to her, so no truancy officers checking in on the kids who weren't in school or registered for home-schooling.

Jess just got to be a mom and take them wherever she wanted. They got to go where they wanted, when they wanted. It was the ideal life, really.

Without the haters. And stupid hashtags directed at her.

Which was why she needed to find her next baby as soon as possible. A baby would be the perfect distraction. People would leave her alone after that, for sure. They'd be so enamored by the newcomer that they'd grow to forget about all the drama. Assuming a new online scandal didn't hit first. People were such sheep. In a month, everyone would forget all about her. Even Alexander would. He'd find some other kid to focus on. One that was actually in danger.

She laughed at the antics on the television as she closed the tabs to her blog and email, then started her search for a baby. It was so easy, really. So many parents posted pictures of their kids publicly. Not only that, but they shared so much about their personal lives it made it easy for Jess to figure out how difficult it would be to snatch the baby.

Some moms posted every little detail, making it so simple to find them. Every Monday was yoga—complete with selfies and humble brags about staying fit as a new mom.

Before too long, she found a few about an hour away. If one didn't work, she could easily go for one of the other two. If all went well, she'd only be gone from the house for a few hours. She didn't like leaving the kids alone, but at least Willow was getting older—she'd be eight soon—and she had a good handle on taking care of the other two. A few hours would be nothing. Willow often took care of the others for longer periods of time when Jess overslept. It was no big deal.

She looked over the pictures of the babies, her heart warming. Soon, she'd be snuggling one of them. Introducing her kids to their newest brother or sister. She was going to try for a boy, but there were never any guarantees. The first two choices were boys but the third was a girl—a darling that looked so much like Daisy, they could actually be sisters. Maybe they would be. Might be for the best. If she brought home a boy, the haters might accuse her of replacing Connor.

Her heart sunk at the thought of him. She tried to push the feelings away.

It didn't work this time. Usually, it did. Maybe because she was so close to having a new baby. Did her heart feel like she was replacing him?

She wasn't! It had been her plan all along to have a big family. Lots of kids, lots of love. All things she'd wanted growing up, but never had. And even better was the fact that she was able to achieve her dream without a man.

It was almost enough for her to reach out to her dad, who said she'd never be anything without a man taking care of her.

But Jess was dead to her parents. Even if she managed to become the queen of England, that wouldn't impress them. They'd still tell her what a horrible person she was.

She needed them like a fish needed a bicycle.

They were dead to her, too.

Jess minimized her browser and looked through photos of Connor. She smiled, laughed, and cried. She'd never missed anyone so much.

But it wasn't the time to focus on that. She made detailed notes so she'd be sure not to make a single misstep.

Now it was a matter of getting a good night's sleep so she would be at the top of her game the next day. There was no room for error. She was going to come home with a baby the next day, no matter what.

VISIT

Alex's pulse drummed in his ears. He and Nick were about to face Dave. The man who had abducted and violated Zoey. He'd thought he was ready but now questioned his sanity.

Nick tapped the table next to him, staring at the door Dave would walk through any minute. Or be shoved through, more likely. Prisoners were rarely happy about being visited by police, although Dave might be the rare exception given how much damage he'd happily inflicted on the families of the two men waiting for him.

Alex wanted to say something, but the silence in the small room was already deafening.

The door jiggled.

He jumped, then sat up straighter and cleared his throat. If Nick noticed Alex's jumpiness, he didn't indicate it. His eyes were still zoned in on the door.

It opened with a scuffle.

Alex's breath hitched. He hadn't seen Dave since the trial, and even then he'd been more focused on Zoey than her captor. The only part of the trial Alex attended was when she'd needed to be there. Beyond that, they focused on healing and moving on. The courtroom only managed to bring them back to a time they wanted to forget.

Dave appeared in a faded blue jumpsuit, chains attached to the cuffs on his wrists and ankles. He looked smaller now. Not that he actually was. Maybe it just seemed that way because Alex and Zoey *had* managed to move on. Or maybe because Alex had made him bigger in his mind. The man who had harmed Zoey, who could potentially take Zander from him. No, not potentially. Theoretically. He'd have to be freed from his multiple life sentences, and there was also the fact that he had no possibility of parole.

The guard shoved him onto a chair across from them and cuffed him to a bar. He looked at Nick and Alex. "I'll be on the other side of the door. Push the button if you need me." Then he glared at Dave. "If you want your time outside today, you'll be on your best behavior in here. Don't forget, you're one wrong move away from solitary. Again."

Dave smirked at Nick. "As long as I get my conjugal."

Nick didn't so much as flinch.

Nobody said a word until the guard left and the door slammed shut.

Dave leaned back in his chair as best as he could with all the chains and cuffs. "What brings you two in?"

Nick leaned forward. "Your son."

"Which one?" Dave sneered.

Alex's palms perspired. He couldn't know about Zander.

"Your only one!" Nick narrowed his eyes. "Mason. Have you been in contact with him?"

"What'd he do now?" Dave sounded bored.

"Don't you know?"

Dave's brows furrowed. "Maybe you've noticed, but they keep me pretty busy in here. Don't get much contact with those outside."

"Mason's in custody."

His smug look faded. "What did he do?"

Nick pressed his palms on the table. "You tell me."

"Don't got a clue. If you don't, either, I'll just go back to my cell. I've got my own, you know. Everyone else has to share, but not me. I got it good here. Even get to see Corrine weekly. Surprised you haven't asked about her."

"You can keep her." Nick stared Dave down. "When was the last time you spoke with Mason?"

"Got me. What month is it now?" He turned to Alex. "May? December? So hard to tell since I ain't got a window."

Alex slammed his fist on the table. "Is that a reference to my wife?"

"Huh?"

"Don't play stupid! May December refers to a relationship with an age gap, you lousy piece of—"

"What do you know about Mason?" Nick interjected. "If you don't tell us what you know, things could get worse for you in here. Or they could get better. Your choice."

Dave yawned. "I already have it pretty good."

Nick's nostrils flared. "We're talking potentially double the outside time and twice the conjugal visits."

"You have my attention."

"What do you know about Mason?" Spittle flew from Nick's mouth.

Dave crossed his arms, kind of. "Honestly, he's not the sharpest knife in the drawer. I mean, really. He should've been able to figure out his relation to Ava."

"Don't utter her name. You can refer to her as my daughter."

"Whatever. You want to know more about Mason or not?"

"Continue." Nick's expression tightened.

"I should probably feel bad about saying my kid ain't all that bright, but they can't all be, you know. You get what you get. Now my other s—"

"Have you been in contact with Mason recently?" Nick shouted.

Alex held his breath. If only Nick had let Dave say one more word, Alex would know if he would've said son or sons. Did the man have any clue about Zander? Alex's mouth tasted like bile.

Dave drew in a deep breath. Held it. Chewed on his lip.

Nick looked like he was about to explode.

"Mason called me on my birthday. Said he was having a great time with his grandparents."

"Don't give me that!" The lines around Nick's eyes were more pronounced. "We both know he's been heading this way for the last year. Taking his slow time, pretending to have a girlfriend— but that could only be a lie, because who'd date that weasel?"

Dave shrugged. "Can't deny that. Why else would he have gone after his own sister?"

"*Half*-sister," Nick corrected.

"Po-tay-to, po-tah-to."

"What has he been planning? Why did he come here?"

Dave gave him a double-take. "He's already in the state?"

"Behind bars."

"You're really not kidding me."

Nick shook his head.

"Kid's acting on his own, whatever he did. Like I said, haven't talked to that dumb piece of crap since my birthday."

"What does he want with Ava?"

"Got me." Dave shrugged.

Silence rested over the room.

Alex leaned over the table. "How many kids have you fathered?"

"Does it matter?"

"Just answer the question."

Dave whispered, then held up one finger. Two. Three.

Alex's heart sank.

"At least three," Dave said. "Hard to say for sure. You know how women are. If they don't like you, they won't tell ya nothin'. I got one ex who swears her kid ain't mine, but the brat is a spitting image of me."

"Who are the three?" Alex squeezed the arms of his chair.

Dave rolled his eyes. "Mason, Parker, and the brat I just told you about."

Alex's body turned to rubber. It took all his strength not to crumple with relief.

"Parker is not yours!" Nick glared at him. "Get that thought out of your head."

Dave grinned. "Corrine says he is. I think she'd know."

"Yet she swore to me he's mine."

"Believe what you want. Don't matter to me none."

Nick's face reddened. "You won't tell us any more about what you and Mason have been discussing?"

Dave shook his head. "I'm done here."

"Then I have no other choice than to suggest your outside time and conjugal visits be cut drastically."

"What?"

Nick rose. "Have fun alone in your cell."

"Wait!"

"See you around." Nicked marched toward the door.

"Stop!" Dave jumped up, but nearly fell because of the chains. "I admit I've been holding out."

Nick turned around. "Have you?"

"Yeah. I'll tell you everything."

"You'd better." Nick sat back down. "Hurry up. I don't have all day."

Dave cleared his throat. "Mason's in love with Ava. I've tried to talk him out of it, but there's no talking the boy out of his feelings. Like you said, though, she's only his *half*-sister. It's not like he likes guys, am I right?"

Alex buried his face in is palms. He was more messed up in the head than Alex had thought all along. And worst of all, this man had supplied half of Zander's gene pool when he'd abducted Zoey. One set of twins, two fathers. The nurse at the hospital had told him it happened more than most people would believe.

Dave's voice pulled Alex from his thoughts. "Mason doesn't want to hurt Ava. The kid just wants her to give him a chance. He's so in love that nothing else matters. I'm sure you know how that feels."

Nick cleared his throat. "You're saying he's come all this way because he's in love?"

"The kid is determined. What can I say?"

"We're done here." Nick rose. "For real, this time. I hope you've told us everything."

"I have! What about my privileges?"

"We'll see." Nick pressed the button, then he and Alex left without another word. On the way out, he stopped at the nearest desk. "When is Dave Cooper's birthday?"

"Let me check." She clacked on her keyboard then looked up. "Four days ago."

Nick muttered under his breath then thanked her for the information.

"He spoke with Mason just four days ago?" Alex exclaimed.

"And he can forget about *all* of his privileges."

"The good news is both of them are behind bars."

"Doesn't make me feel much better," Nick muttered.

They gathered their things then headed for the parking lot. Nick stopped in his tracks staring at his phone.

"What?" Alex tried to see the screen

Nick held it out. "Mason posted bail."

CONFRONTATION

Ava stuffed her phone in a pocket of her bag. She'd fallen asleep early and forgotten to charge her phone the night before. Now it was dead.

At least now she had a good excuse for ignoring Braylon's texts. She was growing less irritated with him but still wasn't ready to talk. Not after he'd gone behind her back to her dad. Sure, she was glad to have Mason in jail, but her boyfriend should've spoken to her first and at least let her know he was thinking about going to her dad.

She glanced around the cafeteria and luckily didn't see Braylon or any of their friends. That would make it easier to grab something to eat and get out of the noisy room. She needed some space to think. There was too much going on, and hardly any time to process any of it—especially between the family meeting the night before and trying to get all her homework done.

Ava made it through the line quickly, ordered a pizza pocket and drink, then made her way outside without running into anyone she was trying to avoid. It was a little cold, which was to her benefit—it meant more kids were staying inside.

She found a tree near the property line and sat at the base, her back to the buildings. Finally, she relaxed. Hidden from everyone and with the next half hour to herself. She took a deep breath before biting into her food.

Her mind raced, going over recent events. First, the meeting the night before. Parker had finally chilled, somewhat at least, and Genevieve had been totally cool. Stepparents got a bad rap, but as long as she didn't have an about-face, she would be the opposite of wicked. They might actually feel like a real family.

Then there was the issue of—

"Oh, there you are," came a familiar male voice on the right.

Ava's heart sank as she turned.

Mason.

Blood drained from her head.

She stared at him, trying to think of something to say. Or to get her feet to run.

He stood not much taller than her, though skinnier and with longer hair. It had been kept short before but now hung over his ears. His stance was that of a hunter awaiting its prey. "You look like you've seen a ghost. Or rather, someone you thought was in jail."

Her eyes widened as she struggled to think of a response. Or a way out. If she grabbed her things and ran, he would have enough time to react and catch her. If she left her stuff, he could go through it. The jerk knew how to hack his way past passcodes.

"Cat got your tongue?"

"How'd you get out?" Her voice wobbled, giving away her worry.

He pursed his lips. "Of jail, you mean?"

"Where else?"

"I came up with the dough."

"How?"

"We can talk about that later."

"You aren't supposed to be here."

"I fit in, don't you think? I'm in high school. Well, I would be if

175

I hadn't dropped out. Who needs school when you can make money delivering packages and giving people rides?"

She rose to her feet and stuffed her shaking hands into her pockets. "What do you want?"

"You." He stared her down.

"Why?"

"I think you know the answer to that."

"Enlighten me." She stepped away from the tree, now hoping one of her friends would find her.

He puckered his lips.

"You're sick."

Mason looked her up and down. "I'm human, and you're a hot little—"

She shoved him. "Shut up! Leave me alone!"

"Are you sure you want to do that? Hanna's wearing a bright green dress today, isn't she?"

Ava tried to remember, but she hadn't been paying attention that morning. "I call BS."

He smirked. "Sure you want to risk it? I know how protective you are of her."

"She's your *sister*! How can you threaten her?"

Mason cocked his brows. "You're my sister, too, and I can guarantee my thoughts about you are much more—"

"Stop!"

He laughed.

"What do you *want*?"

"I already told you."

She clenched her fists. "I have a boyfriend."

"Spoiler alert. He's a loser."

"Takes one to know one."

"So, you admit he's a loser?"

"No! Leave me alone. I don't want anything to do with you. You need to get that through your head! You're nothing to me— not a brother, not a love interest, nothing."

"Ouch."

"Leave me alone! Go away before I call the police."

"They just let me go, or did you already forget? They got nothin' on me."

"Until I tell them you're harassing me."

Mason licked his lips. "I haven't touched you. They can't do squat."

She stepped closer, daring him.

He didn't budge.

"Go back home to your grandparents. There isn't anything here for you. Dave's in prison, and nobody else here wants anything to do with you."

"There's nothing back there for me, either. In case you don't remember, my grandparents can't stand me. Remember when you guys all visited them? I had to stay home."

"I guess I have to give them credit for not being total idiots then, even considering they brought your dad into the world."

He rolled his eyes. "We never got that coffee you promised. Let's get that. Hear me out. You owe me."

Ava shook her head. "I can't leave school until the release bell rings."

Mason panned his palms around. "There's nobody stopping you."

"I already got detention once because of you."

"That just adds to your coolness factor, babe."

She shoved him.

"You know, I'm starting to think maybe I'm the one who needs to file a restraining order on you."

Ava grabbed her bag and slung it over her shoulder. "I need to get to class."

He lifted an eyebrow. "You really care that much about school?"

"Yes, you idiot!"

"That's kinda hot."

She restrained herself from slapping him across the face and stepped around him instead.

He blocked her. "Tell you what."

"You'll leave me alone forever and move back to the bottom of the pond where you belong?"

"I like my women feisty." He grinned. "But no, I'm not going anywhere. It took me long enough to get here. I'm going to make sure it's worth my while."

She stepped back and rolled her eyes, refusing to dignify his stupidity with a response.

Mason crossed his arms. "Okay, here's what's going to happen. I'm going to let you finish your school day. Then you're going to meet me for coffee afterwards. You aren't going to tell anyone about any of this. If you don't show up alone, or at all, or if I'm arrested again, or if anything goes wrong, then Hanna's going to get hurt. I have someone ready to strike at my word, or should I say the lack of my word. If he doesn't hear from me by the time the elementary school lets out, he's going to make his move."

Ava's mouth dropped open. "You're lying."

"Is that a risk you're willing to take?"

She clenched her jaw. He had to be lying, but he was right about her not taking the risk. Not when it came to her innocent baby sister. "Fine. I'll meet you."

"Good."

The bell sounded. She raced toward the school without a word.

"Coffee shop!" he called. "Right after school!"

ATTEMPT

Jess kissed Sammy before laying the sleepy boy in his new toddler bed. The crib would soon belong to the new baby. And if he took a long enough nap, she might be back with the baby before Sammy woke.

Her heart raced at the thought.

She tucked the covers around him then went out to the living room to check on the girls. Daisy was sleeping on the couch and Willow was coloring. Jess carried Daisy to her bed then sat next to her oldest. "You're doing really good with that. Staying in the lines."

"Thanks." Willow didn't look up.

"Your brother and sister are both napping."

Willow nodded, furiously coloring.

"And I think it's almost time to have the baby. Do you know what that means?"

"Yeah. You have to go to the doctor and have him tell you what he thinks."

"Right." Jess kissed her cheek. "So, I need you to watch Sammy and Daisy for me while I do that. If it's time, I'll come back with

STACY CLAFLIN

the baby. If it isn't, then I'll be back and have to go back to the doctor later."

Willow nodded again.

"You okay if I go? You don't need anything?"

"Nope."

"There's some food ready in the fridge if anyone gets hungry. Just take what you need if I'm gone a while."

"'Kay."

"Love you."

"You, too." Willow grabbed a different marker and didn't look up from her page.

Jess gave her another kiss, left the house, then double-checked the lock before starting the car. It was nice to have some time to herself, but she couldn't help worrying about the kids while she was gone. Willow was a great little mom to her siblings, so everything would be fine. She was the most responsible almost-eight-year-old Jess had ever met. She'd make a good actual mom someday.

Once the car was warmed up—it was getting to the point where it needed babying—Jess backed up. She stared at the little house surrounded by woods. Would she be returning with a new baby in a few hours?

A warmth spread through her, and she had a good feeling. This was going to be her day. Maybe she'd even get the first baby she attempted. She'd never been that lucky before. Even as easy as it had been to take Sammy over a year ago—his DNA supplier had leaped across the park to her older kids, leaving him right next to her—Jess had already had three failed attempts.

No matter how you went about it, having a baby was not easy. Especially not like this. But it was worth it in the end. There wasn't anything like holding her sweet babies right after she got them.

She triple-checked the address in the GPS, then headed down the gravel driveway, which led to a dirt road. Then finally pave-

180

ment. Sometimes it was a pain living off the beaten path, but it kept them from dealing with nosy neighbors or anyone ever accidentally finding them.

The drive was pretty quick, as it was early enough in the day to miss any traffic issues. She arrived at the beach and looked around. Hardly anyone there. Hopefully, the baby would be there. The mom hadn't posted any social media updates indicating an outing to the shore that day. But maybe she'd just arrived. Didn't matter either way. This was only one of three potential babies. She still had a good feeling about returning home with a bundle of joy.

Jess slid on her long red wig and added her signature floppy hat and big sunglasses. At least nobody would question the hat and sunglasses at the beach. It was overcast, but still bright. The kind of day people got sunburned because they didn't bother with sunscreen and didn't realize how many of the sun's rays were actually bouncing off the water.

After double-checking her appearance, she slid out of the car and quickly adjusted the fake belly. Once everything was perfect, she trekked over the grassy hill until she came to the sandy, rocky shore. Lazy waves splashed, and a toddler sat burying her legs in the sand while her mom fussed over a baby in one of those wrap things.

It was hard to tell from the distance, but it looked like her woman. If not, these people would do. The baby looked small enough—not that she needed a newborn. Just one young enough that wouldn't make Willow start asking questions. She was getting smarter by the day, and Jess couldn't placate her with pat answers anymore.

She made her way over and stopped to say hi to the toddler first. The little girl giggled and said she was a mermaid, pointing to the wet sand over her legs that was supposed to be a tail.

"Wow, I've never met a real mermaid before." Jess smiled

widely then headed for the mom, who was glued to her phone. "How'd you manage a mermaid for a daughter?"

"Huh?" The woman looked up. "Oh, yeah. She's obsessed."

"How old's the little one?" Jess nodded to the baby, mentally planning how to get her with the challenge of being attached to the mom.

"Seven weeks." She smiled. "When are you due?"

Jess put her hands on her back and gave a little groan. "Today, actually. I'm hoping that walking around will help kick things into gear, you know?"

"Good luck with that. Hasn't worked for me. I tried everything both times, and each time they came two weeks late."

"So the second one doesn't come earlier?"

"Not for me." The woman turned back to her phone.

"See you around." Jess turned around and walked back the way she came, stopping when she reached the little girl again. She squatted and whispered, "Have you played in the water yet? It's the perfect day for it."

"Mama said I can't." She patted her 'tail' and added more sand.

"It isn't that bad."

The toddler gave her a quizzical expression.

"Really. The water's so calm, you'd easily be able to find starfish and sand dollars. Have you ever seen those before?"

"Yep."

"You should go look."

The mom was staring at Jess, her head tilted. Probably didn't trust her. Everyone was so distrusting these days.

Jess started to rise. "You really should go look. I heard there are mermaids out there on days like this."

The little girl snapped her attention to Jess. "Really?"

"Yeah. I'd look, but I can't go in the water right now." Jess started to walk away, but gave the toddler an encouraging expression.

She didn't head for the water, but did stare at it with a conflicted expression.

Jess held back a smile and silently willed the girl to go. Then she could make her move. Get the baby and get out of there.

The mom was still watching Jess.

She put her hands back around her waist and trudged toward the water. That might be all the encouragement the girl would need to go looking for mermaids. Distract the kid, who would distract the mom. It was all Jess needed to make her move.

But the kid didn't budge. Just sat there patting down the sand over her legs.

Jess shoved aside her frustration. She just needed to think of something, anything, that would work. Maybe she could convince the little girl to run off to the playground without telling her mom. Or to the tall logs near the docks. Then Jess could offer to hold the baby while Mom rushed off to help the toddler.

It had worked so well with getting Sammy. Surely, it'd work now. A seven-week-old would be the perfect addition to her family.

Jess made a dramatic production of walking along the shoreline, grasping her back and rubbing her belly. The child hadn't budged, but the mom was now closer to her, going back and forth between watching Jess and interacting with her phone.

Maybe this wasn't her lucky day, after all. Or maybe this was the wrong baby. She'd give it one more try before moving to the next one.

Jess wandered back over to them. She smiled at the mom. "Still nothing."

"Probably isn't time yet." She gave an obviously forced smile.

"I'm determined to have this baby on the due date."

"Like I said, good luck with that."

Jess turned to the little girl. "I think I saw a mermaid in the water."

Her eyes lit up. "You did?"

The mom's nostrils flared. "Come on, Maddie. We're leaving."

"But, Mommy!"

"Now." She flung the sandy toys into the diaper bag, grabbed the child, and stormed toward the parking lot with the girl on her hip.

Jess crossed her arms. So much for that.

Time to try again.

WORRY

Nick slammed his phone on the desk. Every time he called Ava, the call went straight to voicemail. She should've been out of school, which meant she needed to answer his calls. That was part of the deal to keep the device. And he needed to make sure she'd gotten his texts about Mason being out. She hadn't responded to any of them.

Then he checked on the officer posted at her school. She hadn't gotten on the bus. He'd already reported it, but it hadn't made it to Nick's desk. After vowing to find out who was responsible for that mess-up, he called the school to make sure she had even shown up that day.

"Let me check the records." Typing sounded on the other side of the phone. "Yes, she was at all of her classes, but I see that she didn't show up at the tryouts for the play."

"She was going to try out for a play?"

"According to this. She'd signed up to try out after school today."

"There isn't anywhere she'd be? Like, detention?"

"No. I'm sorry, Captain Fleshman."

"Call me if you hear from her."

"Of course."

"Thanks." Nick ended the call and tugged on his hair. Assuming she wasn't in a ditch somewhere—which was a lot better than he was actually picturing—he would give her the lecture of a lifetime. Probably take away phone privileges.

Unfortunately, with Mason out on bail, chances were she was with him and his worst fears were likely to be reality.

He'd sent every free officer out to look for him, but so far, nobody had seen a thing.

It was time for him to get out there. Being captain, he was usually expected to be at the station, but this was one of those times that called for him to be out in the field. No way was he going to sit this one out now that Ava had missed her afterschool tryout.

He gathered his things and updated everyone on the situation, then grabbed the first officer he saw to join him.

"Me, sir?" Chang asked.

They'd been at odds for some time, and that was undoubtedly why the other man was leaving the force soon. Alex would be a much more pleasant day shift replacement. "Yeah. Come on."

Chang followed Nick to his Mustang then they hit the street. He asked questions about Ava and Mason as Nick drove.

The first place he went was the school. Neither of them was anywhere in sight. Then he headed for the coffee shop where he'd arrested the little pervert. But they weren't in there, either.

He told Chang to call it in and see if there were any new updates.

"None, Captain."

Nick frowned. With so many on the lookout, someone had to see something. But it was anyone's guess where Mason would take Ava. Could be anywhere, but he didn't have the advantage of being from around the area. It was a small enough town, though growing, and most everyone on the force had grown up here.

His stomach churned acid. It lurched. His chest tightened.

He wanted to hunt down the person who had posted Mason's bail. Who would do such a thing? His attorney? Or did the kid actually have a girlfriend? But if that were the case, why would she be helping him with Ava? Either the girlfriend was as twisted as Mason, or she had no clue what he was actually doing.

Nick had seen enough cases of male-female criminal teams to know it was a possibility the kid had found someone crazy enough to work with him to hunt down Ava and help him to finish what he'd started more than a year earlier.

"You okay, Captain?" Chang's voice pulled Nick from his thoughts.

He realized his knuckles were turning white from squeezing the steering wheel. "I'll be okay once I know my daughter's safe."

"Can you think of anywhere else she might be?"

"If I could, don't you think I'd have looked?"

"I'm just thinking, your daughter is tough. And when I interviewed the kid, he wasn't all that bright. It wouldn't surprise me if she took control of the situation and convinced him to go somewhere she'd have the upper hand."

Nick stopped at a light and turned to him. "You really think so?"

"Yeah. I'm not saying Cooper isn't dangerous, but your daughter could easily work him. Turn the situation to her advantage. She got away from him the first time he assaulted her, didn't she? When they were back East with your ex?"

"That's true, but I don't trust Mason. He traveled all the way here just for Ava. No other purpose."

"And his dad didn't say anything when you went to interview him?"

"I should've pushed him harder. Dave kept saying he hadn't talked to Mason since his birthday. Then I found out his birthday was four days ago."

"He's in on it. Want to go back to the prison and interrogate him? I'll call and let them know we're on our way."

Nick's heart pumped harder. He'd love nothing more than to grab Dave by the collar and choke him, but interrogating him would have to do. "Let's do that. Thanks."

"Don't thank me until his kid is behind bars again and your daughter's safe."

Nick turned down a side street and headed for the freeway. He was going to the penitentiary for the second time that day.

TRAP

Ava sat across from Mason and glared at him. "I want proof that Hanna's okay."

He shoved a white paper cup in front of her. "I don't have her. How am I supposed to do that?"

She balled her fists and leaned over the table. "Find a way! You have someone watching her. The dude who was going to act if you didn't contact him."

"Her," Mason corrected. "And she already left."

"Get me proof!"

He narrowed his eyes. "You don't get to call the shots!"

"If you want me to hear you out, I do. Show me she's safe, and you have my attention."

Mason muttered something under his breath.

"What was that?"

"You're supposed to be shaking in your boots, not ordering me around. You don't seem to get how this is going to go."

"I only came here to protect my sister. You don't convince me she's safe, we don't have a deal."

"That's not what we agreed on."

"I'll scream. Everyone will turn and look. Some people are bound to recognize me as the police captain's daughter."

He leaned back and folded his arms. "I'll call the chick. Then the subject is dropped. Got it? You can ask my friend if she's okay."

"I said *proof*. A picture of her getting on the bus or safe at my grandparents' house. Something like that."

Mason pulled out his phone. "Fine. Then you're doing what I say."

"Whatever."

"Drink your coffee."

She eyed it. "What'd you spike it with?"

He glared at her. "Nothing. I don't have a lot of money and I don't want it to go to waste."

Ava bit back a sarcastic comment and brought the cup to her mouth, but she didn't sip it. She took a deep breath but didn't smell anything weird. Not that it meant anything. Plenty of drugs were odorless.

"You got proof the brat's fine?" Mason said into the phone.

She kicked him for calling Hanna a brat.

He knitted his brows together, giving her a frightening look that sent an icy chill down her spine. His eyes seemed hollow, empty. Like he lacked a soul.

A minute later, he ended the call then showed her his screen. A photo of Hanna lined up at her school bus.

Her stomach twisted. It creeped her out that someone was watching her nine-year-old sister. Someone working with or for Mason.

"Happy?"

Not being stuck here with you. She gave a slight nod. "What do you want from me?"

"I think you know." He nodded to her drink. "You drank that yet?"

"It's delicious," she lied. "Why am I here?"

"You really don't know?"

"Would I keep asking if I did?"

They stared each other down before he spoke. "You know how I feel about you."

She flashed back to him groping her at the Halloween party. "You really should get help for that."

"Why? You so clearly feel the same way."

Her mouth dropped open. "Say what?"

"Don't try to deny it."

"Maybe you haven't noticed, but I have a boyfriend."

"The guy you aren't speaking to?" Mason leaned forward.

Her stomach dropped. He knew about that? She struggled to find her voice. "You're wrong. And even if that were true, what makes you think I'd want you?"

"You never pressed charges. You had the chance, but you didn't do it."

The coffee shop seemed to shrink around her, press on her. "Because I thought it was a mistake! That you were high on something. I just didn't want to ruin your life. A charge like that won't go away. *That* was what I was thinking. I was trying to be nice!"

A slow smile spread across his face. "So, you do like me."

"I was trying to protect my brother!"

"Really?" He rested his chin on his palm. "We didn't know we were related back then. Remember?"

"You were about to become my stepbrother, Mason. I've always thought of you as a brother. That's it. Nothing more. Don't you realize how gross it is for brothers and sisters to hook up?"

"Half-siblings. Only half."

Ava ran her fingers through her hair. It would take a miracle to get through to him.

Think!

She turned her head toward the door. "Is that my dad?"

"What?" Mason spun around.

191

Ava swapped their drinks then brought his up to her mouth like she was sipping it.

He turned back and glared at her. "I don't see him."

She glanced at the door. "My mistake. That guy looked like him."

"The Samoan dude?"

"No. The other one. But seriously, can I go? I met you. We talked. I'm late for a play tryout."

"I suppose you're going to blame that on me, just like missing detention?"

Ava set the cup down. "Well, it isn't anyone else's fault."

His face reddened. "I don't want to spend any more time here. This is probably the first place your dad would look."

"Since this is where he arrested you."

Mason's nostrils flared. "Just drink your coffee. We're leaving in a minute."

Ava picked up the cup and sniffed it as she brought it to her mouth. Just smelled like a mocha. At least once they left the coffee shop, it would be easier to get away. Now that she knew Hanna was okay, she could make her move.

She sipped the warm, chocolatey drink and smiled as Mason drank the coffee meant for her.

Lucky for her, he was an idiot.

He set the cup down. "You know, I've been dreaming of this day for a long time. More and more since I've been on my way here. The wait has been worth it, Aves. You—"

"Don't use that nickname!" She set her cup down. "That's what my mom calls me. You don't get to use it, understand?"

Was it her imagination or was her tongue not quite working right? A few of her words sounded a little off.

Mason shrugged. "Fine by me. I'll come up with something that's special. Just between you and me. Something no one else uses."

A strange feeling swept through her, massaged her. For a moment, it seemed like water waved between them.

Ava swore. She hadn't meant to do that out loud.

Mason leaned forward. "Feeling a little funny?"

She tried to pull some hair behind her ear, but missed and poked her eye. "What'd you do?"

He smirked. "I put something in my drink, Aves dear."

His drink.

"I knew you wouldn't drink from the one I handed you. See how well I know you? It's a shame you don't trust me." He rose and helped her up. "Let's get you out of here before you really start to get tipsy."

She tried to object. The words didn't reach her mouth.

DISCOVERY

Alex's vision grew bleary. He sat back and rubbed his eyes. He'd been studying pictures on the mommy blogger's blog for hours, spending as much time as he could on each individual one. He'd zoomed them in as much as possible, taking in every tiny detail hoping to find a clue previously missed.

So far, nothing.

"You're not dressed?"

Alex looked up at Zoey then at the time. "I'm going to be late!" He scurried out of the chair and raced over to the closet, donning his uniform as fast as possible.

"Do you need me to do anything?" she asked.

His mind raced. "Can you throw together something for me to eat?"

"Sure thing." Zoey hurried out of the room.

He ran around, getting ready, and nearly bumped into Zoey as he opened the door.

"Sorry." She smiled and handed him a sack lunch.

He gave her a quick kiss. "You're a lifesaver! Thank you."

"Need anything else?"

"Just tell the kids goodnight for me and that I love them."

"Will do." She fixed his hair and kissed him. "Have a good night at work."

"I'll try." He bolted for the door.

"Alex!"

He spun around. "I'm going to be late."

She disappeared then reappeared holding a travel coffee mug. "I know it's not a peppermint mocha, but at least it's coffee."

His insides melted. "You made me coffee?"

"With mint creamer. Love you." She handed it to him then gave him one last kiss.

"You make it hard to leave for work."

Her eyes twinkled. "Maybe we can have some fun tomorrow."

His pulse raised. "I could always call in sick."

She batted her eyelashes. "I'll be here when you get back."

Alex forced himself to open the door before he convinced himself to stay home. He wouldn't be able to hide the truth from his boss if he did call in. Not when the captain was his best friend.

He sipped the minty coffee as he rushed toward his car and pulled away as soon as the engine turned on. Maybe he needed to set an alarm so he wouldn't lose track of time like that again. Anything to avoid a rush out the door like that. At least he had Zoey, or he'd probably still be staring at the screen.

Everything was quiet at the station. Hardly anyone was there. Alex went back to the reception desk. "Everyone out on a call?"

"You didn't hear?" Mary's eyes filled with concern.

"Did I miss something that was all over the news?"

She shook her head, her mouth curving down. "The captain's daughter is missing."

"What?" Alex exclaimed. "Mason posted bail! It has to be him."

Her frown deepened. "Most everyone is out looking for them. The captain included."

Alex's pulse drummed in his ears. "Are there any clues?"

She shook her head. "Not that I'm aware of."

He scrambled back to his desk, calling Nick.

"You on duty now?" Nick asked.

"Yeah. Mary just told me what happened. Why didn't you let me know? I'd have come in early. You know I would've. I'm on my way out now."

"Actually, I have something for you to do there."

"You don't want me on this?" Disappointment washed through Alex.

"We just discovered Mason has a relative in the area."

"Yeah. Your kids."

"Other than the obvious. No, a distant cousin. We think he might be helping Mason. I need you to look into him."

"Whatever you need."

"I'll send you what I know." Nick ended the call.

Alex raced to his desk and turned on his laptop. The message came in and Alex got to work. It was no wonder he wanted Alex on this job. He'd gotten really good at finding information online, and even more so with the resources of the station.

It took him almost no time to discover where Mason's third cousin lived and that he had a cabin not far away. Why was it always a cabin in the woods?

Alex sent Nick everything he found, then he closed the tab. His screen showed a post from the mommy blogger he'd been looking at before. He was about to close that, too, when something in a picture made him stop cold.

He zoomed in on the picture. It had a car in the background, the license plate visible but blurry.

Could that be her car? The clue he'd been searching for all along? His heart pounded like a jackhammer as he used a software program to focus in on the plate. Even with the expensive, advanced program Alex was only able to make out some of the numbers.

But it was more than he had before. Between that and the make and model of the car, he could narrow it down significantly.

Maybe even find the exact car in the database before he finished his coffee.

Maybe they could capture Mason and the mommy blogger in one night. It was a lot to ask, but at this point, it wasn't out of the question.

Alex couldn't believe his eyes when he saw the results. There weren't *any* matches for the plate and car type and color. Nothing.

He ran it again. Extending out the area.

Still nothing. Not one match.

He turned back to the picture and made some guesses as to what the unidentifiable numbers and letters could be. Then he ran those through the system.

After coming up blank again, he tried without the make, model, and color of the car.

Bingo.

Four possible matches. One plate belonged to an elderly man in a nursing home. That left three more.

Alex's fingers shook as he looked into the remaining ones. The next belonged to a thirty-something woman in Portland.

That was promising.

Except that she was in Africa on a missionary trip building orphanages, and had been for the last year and a half.

Two more.

A basketball coach in Spokane. The plate belonged to a brand new pickup truck.

Alex drew in a deep breath and held it. Would the last one be a dead end, or exactly what he was looking for?

The plate belonged to a twenty-eight-year-old woman named Elizabeth Jessica McAdams. She was single and had no kids.

Alex's heart sunk. Another dead end. The woman had no kids. No address, either. Not only that, but the car matching the plate had been demolished after a collision several years before. Couldn't be the same plate.

Or could it?

It was possible, but without being able to clearly see the entire string of numbers and letters, there was no way to tell for certain.

That would have to wait. Alex needed to get back to looking into Mason. That was what he'd been doing before he accidentally saw the car.

Alex called Nick to find out if he needed any help.

"Chang and I are heading over to the cabin," Nick said. "Sanchez and Mackey are checking out the primary residence. Be ready to provide back-up for whoever finds something."

"So, you just want me to sit and wait?"

"Basically. Be ready to head over here if I call."

"I was born ready. Oh, and Nick?"

"Yeah?"

"Ava will be fine. She's tough."

"Thanks. We've got to put Mason away for good. Between him and his dad, they've caused her three lifetimes worth of trauma."

"He's going down. No doubt about it."

They ended the call and Alex took his cup to the coffee machine and poured himself some more. As much as he wanted to be out there helping to find Ava, at least it gave him more time to look into the blogger.

Someone needed to find out what really happened to Connor. The kid needed an advocate, or at least justice—depending on if he was still alive.

Back at his desk, Alex looked into Elizabeth. There was nothing of interest beyond the fact that she'd gone off the grid. She did have an ex-husband, but they'd had no kids. There was nothing to link her to Connor.

He nursed his coffee and went back to the blog. The answers were there, they were just hidden. It was only a matter of finding them.

Alex scrolled, studied pictures, scrolled some more, and checked his phone for updates from Nick.

He was just about to take a break and stretch his legs when he saw something that made him freeze. It was a picture of the blogger's youngest son as a baby. Something about the tiny face was familiar. And not because he'd spent enough time looking at the posts to make himself go cross-eyed.

He'd seen that face somewhere else, not on her blog.

But where?

Alex tapped his desk and strained to recall where he'd seen that face.

Then he remembered.

He nearly knocked his cup over as he scrambled to pull up his blog. Then he went back to the beginning and scanned the posts in the order he'd published them.

Then he came to a post from about a year and a half earlier. The details were fuzzy at first, but as he read his own words, it all came crashing back.

The baby's mom had contacted him in a frenzy. A woman had run off from a park with her son when she'd gotten distracted with her other two kids.

Alex's mouth dried as he compared the pictures from his blog and the mommy blogger's. The mommy blogger had announced her child's birth just two days after the baby had been taken from the park. She didn't post any pictures of Sammy's face for nearly six months.

Probably to keep anyone from recognizing the baby. He'd changed a lot in that time, as babies do. But it was the same boy. Of that, Alex was certain.

To double-check if his memory served correctly, he went through other old posts on the mommy blog. Sure enough, the woman didn't post any baby faces until about six months after announcing the arrivals.

She'd kidnapped all four of them.

And one was missing without a viable explanation. The custody change story was even more suspicious now.

Alex stared at the screen as his mind filled in all the blanks.

Everything made sense with this new knowledge. The lack of pictures at hospitals and doctor visits. No pictures of her face. The lack of baby pictures for the first six months.

The only question still remaining was what had happened to Connor. Had she moved from child abduction to murder?

Then a sickening thought hit him.

She was posting about pregnancy. Claiming to be close to birth.

Another baby was going to be kidnapped soon.

He needed to stop her.

Alex reached for his laptop. Just as he did, Nick called for Alex's help.

The blogger would have to wait.

CONSEQUENCES

Jess slunk onto the couch and emptied the full wine glass. It had taken everything in her to hide her frustration from the kids. They were bummed about not having the baby home yet, but had been easily distracted when she streamed a new movie for them.

Three babies, and she didn't manage to get any of them. Three!

Was she losing her touch? Picking the wrong people? Or were moms wising up?

She needed to come up with a better plan. Something where she controlled more of the variables. There had been too many people around for her to try and snatch the second one. And the third lady hadn't been where she'd posted she was going to be.

Days like this were the worst.

And she was exhausted and stressed out. The last thing she wanted to do was cook up a new plan. All she wanted to do was climb into bed and have a good cry. Life would've been so much easier if she could just have kids naturally. Or if she hadn't been disqualified for adoption.

It hadn't been her fault. She'd been babysitting when her boyfriend at the time had come over. Everything had been going fine until he'd given his peanut butter granola bar to one of the kids when Jess hadn't been looking. The kid had a peanut allergy and the house had been nut-free. He hadn't known, and she didn't know he'd had the bar with him.

Once the girl's face swelled and changed colors, he ran. Didn't even tell Jess what had happened. By the time she'd found the girl, it had been too late. The whole thing had been a nightmare. Jess had never wanted anything to happen to the girl and her boyfriend denied ever being at the house.

Luckily for her, the attorney had been able to prove he was there. Even got Jess out of serving any jail time. But part of the condition was that she could never work with kids again. Child endangerment was on her permanent record. It had broken her heart then. For as long as she could remember, she'd wanted to have kids and work with them. They were her life and part of every dream she ever had for herself.

Tears blurred her vision. Guilt still tore at her for the little girl's death. It was her fault. She should've told her boyfriend about the allergy as soon as he stepped inside. But she hadn't, and an innocent child had paid the price. A family lived with the heartache.

And she was certain that was why she no longer had Connor. It was a cosmic payback. Karma alive and well. She'd avoided jail, but not the consequences of what she'd done. Now she lived with the same pain she had caused another mom.

Jess wiped her eyes then went into Connor's room. Her original plan had been for Sammy to share the room with Connor, but with him gone, she hadn't been able to bring herself to move Sammy. She wouldn't even let the other kids in there.

It was all she had left of Connor. Except for the small grave out back. The kids had asked about the disturbed dirt, and she'd told them she'd found a dead coyote and buried it. They'd believed her.

She sat on Connor's bed and hugged Willy, his favorite teddy bear. Hot tears stung her eyes. She sobbed, shaking, soaking the stuffed animal. "I'm sorry, Connor. I never meant for it to happen."

His sweet smile appeared in her mind. She could almost feel his arms around her. What she wouldn't give to actually feel them. To hold him one more time. To feel his silky hair against her face and to hear his contagious giggles.

Connor's smile melted away to the scene that haunted her nightmares. Waking to find him lying on the kitchen floor. Unmoving. Eerily pale. His little hands resting on his neck.

He'd been going through a growth spurt and was always asking for food. The only thing that made sense was that he'd gotten up for a midnight snack and choked. Hadn't come to her for help. Probably afraid he'd get in trouble for sneaking food.

If only he'd known she wouldn't have cared! She only wanted him alive.

Even though she knew it was too late, she'd tried to remove the food. Lifted him up and pushed up under his diaphragm. The half-chewed donut flew across the room, not that it did any good.

Sobbing, she took him outside and dug the tiny hole, covering him before the other kids had a chance to see him. She couldn't let them know what had happened to him. They were too young for such heartache.

By the time they woke up, Jess had concocted a story about him going on a trip. Said she didn't know when he'd be back. Figured they'd eventually stop asking.

They hadn't, but they asked a lot less these days.

She wiped her tears away, then headed for her computer. It was time to focus on the future, not the past. Time to find her next baby.

And her next attempt *would* be successful.

TRAPPED

S omething poked Ava, waking her. She rolled over, pushing aside her blankets. No, not hers. She'd never seen them before, and they reeked of musk. Unlike the air, which smelled like burning candles and air freshener. Soft music played somewhere.

"Ava," the male voice whispered.

At first, she thought it was Parker.

"Ava…"

Wrong brother.

She bolted up.

Mason brushed some hair away from her eyes. "Did you sleep well, sweet angel?"

"Shut up." She shoved him. "Where are we?"

"Far, far away from the rest of the world. It's just the two of us."

"Where did you bring me?" Ava demanded.

"Relax. I didn't go all 'Dad' on you. You're not locked up, are you?" He stepped back, and that's when she noticed he was wearing a dress shirt and a tie. "Look at this place—this isn't the family's abandoned shack."

She glanced around. White Christmas lights lined the ceiling. Candlelight bounced around the walls covered with cheap-looking paintings. Rose petals were spread across the bed, not doing anything to make the thin, pilling comforter look any better. Pictures of them together were hung around the room.

"Does this look like a torture chamber?" He cupped her chin. "Although we can go there if you want."

Ava pulled away. "What did you do to me while I was sleeping?"

"Nothing. I was busy setting all this up." He panned his palms around the room. "I hope you like it. Are you hungry? Dinner's ready. You have excellent timing."

Her stomach rumbled at the thought of food. Then she flashed back to the coffee shop. She shook her head. "Take me home."

Mason shook his head. "I want you to give us a chance."

"And I want to go home."

"You're not being held against your will."

She gave him a double-take.

"I didn't restrain you. You can walk out that door any time."

Ava jumped to her feet.

He rose also. "But you won't get very far without your shoes. I have a car. Give me a chance, then I'll take you home if you really want."

Ava glanced down at her feet. Her blood-red nail polish confirmed she really was barefoot.

Mason walked around to her side of the bed and held out a hand. "Come on. What's the harm in dinner and a movie? If we get started now, you might not even miss curfew."

Her stomach twisted. Dad had to be so worried. "I need to call my dad and let him know I'm okay."

"He'll know when you show up. Come on." He inched closer, reaching for her hand.

She didn't budge.

"The sooner we start, the sooner I'll offer to take you home."

STACY CLAFLIN

Ava stared into his eyes, trying to decide if she believed him. He'd drugged her to bring her here—wherever *here* was—so what were the chances he'd actually take her home if she did cooperate?

He grabbed her hand. His was entirely too smooth. "Let's eat."

Her mind raced. She should run for the door. He had said she was free to go. But she'd fare a lot better if she had her shoes. Maybe she should find those first. Play along, then bolt at a more opportune time.

And hope it wasn't a trap. She'd deal with that later. Give him a few minutes to make him think he could trust her. Then she'd make her move.

She followed him until he stopped in front of a closed door. Her heart jumped into her throat. What was behind the door? Beads of sweat broke out along her hairline as she flashed back to Dave's cabin in the woods. Being locked in a tiny bedroom. Great, she was going to need therapy again. These Cooper men were determined to keep her there.

Mason tilted his head. "Nervous? Don't be." He shoved open the door to reveal a candlelit bathroom. "Take a few minutes to get ready. I have a dress for you to change into. Once you're set, we can have dinner. I made your favorite."

"My favorite?"

He nodded. "You always ordered the same thing when we went out to eat for family night with Mom and Dad. Go ahead, but don't take too long."

She stepped inside and closed the door, relieved to be out of his presence, even if it was only for a few minutes. And it would only be a few minutes. There was no window. But there were more pictures of them.

Ava went to the bathroom and wracked her mind for ideas. If she came up with a dozen escape plans, maybe one would work. It wasn't getting out that worried her as much as getting away. She'd gotten *out* of Dave's cabin. But he'd brought her back in.

If Ava was going to get away, she needed to be sure she could.

Mason could've been lying about them not being back in the same cabin. Sure, it looked different now, but that didn't mean anything. She hadn't seen all of the cabin.

Or it could be a different one altogether. Who was to say Dave didn't have a stockpile of cabins?

Knock, knock!

"Almost done in there? Don't want the food to get cold for you."

She bit back a retort. "Just a minute!"

"I'll be waiting."

Her stomach turned. At least he was smaller than his dad.

She could fight him off. And she would.

But first she needed to pretend to go along with his plan. Find her shoes, her phone. Call for help as she ran. That would be ideal. But she would flee barefoot if she had to.

Ava finally looked at the dress hanging on the back of the door. It was surprisingly modest. She'd have expected something dark, skin-tight, and low-cut. It was pale pink and flowy. Delicate.

Seriously? He was trying to turn her into a dainty, fragile lady? She started to laugh, but quickly covered her mouth. At least she knew what role to play. How to stroke his ego and get her to trust him before getting away.

"How's it going in there?"

She grabbed the dress. "Almost done. I love the dress."

"You do? I mean, wonderful! How does it look on you?"

She slid off her clothes. "Like you wouldn't believe."

"Perfect. The table's set."

Ava pulled on the dress and slid two sparkling rose clips sitting next to the sink into her hair.

Then she opened the door.

STAKEOUT

Nick's pulse drummed in his ear. They were almost at the cabin. Only about five minutes out, maybe ten, if the terrain kept getting more difficult. The hill was growing steeper with each step, and the thorns thicker.

Alex whacked more vines. "Doesn't look like anyone's been out here in years. Sure we have the right place?"

"I'm sure there's a dirt road we weren't able to find. They might drive in from the other side of the forest. Hard to say, but I'm not giving up."

"Should you even be here? Conflict of interest and all that."

The unspoken truth hung between them—they both knew all too well about conflict of interest. Nick hated it, but knew it was for the best. "I'm only here to see Ava with my own two eyes once she's brought out safe and sound."

"And to see Mason arrested."

"For good this time."

Alex nodded then whacked some more vines from the path.

The cabin came into view. The full moon cast a glow on it, giving them a decent view despite the time of night.

Nick's breath hitched.

Alex lifted a brow, then called it in.

It took all of Nick's self-control to stay in place. His firstborn was inside. Her older half-brother was doing who-knew-what to her. Nick had a few ideas, and each of them made his blood boil.

"Sanchez, Mackey, and Garcia are almost here. We should wait for them."

"What have they found?"

"Nothing useful."

Nick gritted his teeth. "Can't send you in alone."

Alex nodded. "I'm going to look around."

"And I'll be close by."

Alex put his knife away, pulled out his pistol, then crept toward the tiny building.

Nick grabbed his gun, ready to stop Mason. He followed Alex, staying back. From where he stood, the cabin looked empty. Dark. No lights shone from the windows. That didn't mean anything. Mason could've put up blackout curtains. Or could've simply been on the other side of the house.

Or not there.

He shoved that thought from his mind. That wasn't an option. Ava was inside, end of story. They were about to go in and rescue her, then Nick would bring her home while Mason got arrested again.

Then the whole thing would be behind them. At least until the trial. But Mason would be behind bars, and they could all focus on the wedding.

Just as Alex rounded the other side of the cabin, a voice sounded behind Nick. He pointed in the direction Alex had just gone. Garcia followed him, and the other officers went around the other side. Nick's stomach knotted. What he wouldn't give to be with them instead of just watching, waiting.

It was *his* baby girl inside with a lunatic.

Some others from the force arrived. He again pointed toward the cabin, hating more than before the fact that he couldn't take part. At least he knew Ava was in good hands. He trusted his brothers and sisters in blue with both his life and Ava's. They knew what was at stake.

Nick kept his weapon ready as he paced, listening. Waiting.

Doing nothing.

Bang!

His stomach plummeted.

Then his heart raced. Was his daughter's attacker down?

He resisted the urge to bolt around the building.

Listened. Checked the radio.

Nothing.

Silence rang through the air louder than the bullet fired.

Alex reappeared. The moonlight made it look like he was covered in blood.

Nick ran to him. "What happened?"

He shook his head.

"What does that mean?" Nick exclaimed. Terror tore through him. "Was Ava shot?"

Alex wiped his face. "The cabin was empty. Well mostly."

"What do you mean?"

"There was a family of raccoons. A rabid one jumped down on me from a rafter. That was the shot you heard. It's raccoon blood covering me."

It took a moment for it to sink in. "She's not in there?"

Alex shook his head. "The building has been cleared."

"Are you okay?"

He nodded. "I might need stitches. Probably a rabies shot."

"Let's get you back to the car." Nick headed for the path they'd cleared.

Where was his daughter, if not at the cabin?

SHOCK

Ava scowled as Mason scooted her chair in. As soon as he sat across from her she smiled as sweetly as she could muster. "I can't believe you went to all this trouble for me."

"You deserve nothing other than the best." His gaze roved over her. "And you look angelic. Even better than I pictured when I picked out that dress."

She threw up in her mouth a little. "You have great taste."

Like the bile on her tongue.

"Are your arms okay? Those scabs look painful." He winced as if he actually cared.

Ava smiled. "It's nothing."

He poured some champagne into her cup, then filled his. "Dish up. I made it all for you."

Ava batted her lashes as she swallowed the puke. She scooped some fettuccine Alfredo onto the plate in front of her.

"You can take more."

"I don't want to stuff myself."

His mouth formed a pout. "But it's for you."

"Aren't you going to have any?"

"Of course. But dish yourself more."

She bit her tongue and piled on more noodles. "This really is enough."

He nodded, his pout disappearing, then he piled his plate with the pasta. While he did that, Ava scooped some salad and vegetables next to her fettuccine. He had gone all out. Maybe he really did just want to woo her.

Mason glanced up at her. She immediately started chewing, pretending she'd already dug in. The aromas made her mouth water and her stomach rumble. As soon as she saw him eat from the same dishes she'd taken her food, she would eat.

She willed him to take a bite.

He didn't touch his fork. "How do you like it?"

Ava swallowed. "Better than that little Italian place we used to go to."

His eyes lit up. "Really?"

She closed her eyes and moaned. "So much better."

The loser was beaming when she opened her eyes. "Wow, and on my first try! Just think how much better it'll be after I've made it a few times."

Ava forced a smile. "Try it."

He shook his head. "I want to watch you."

Her heart pounded so hard she swore he could hear it across the table. "I don't want to be selfish."

"You aren't." He gestured for her to eat.

Ava's hands shook. What would he do if she refused? Worse, what would happen if she actually ate some? He could've spiked it like the coffee.

Mason nodded, unblinking.

"If you insist." She reached for the fork, still shaky, and twirled some noodles around it.

He leaned forward, his eyes widening.

She imagined stabbing him with the fork and making her getaway. Instead, she brought the food to her mouth. Glanced between him and the pasta. Opened her mouth. Her mouth watered again despite her trepidation.

Mason stared, his lips pursing.

Ava pretended to bite down, her lips brushing the sauce but not actually getting anything into her mouth. She dropped the fork and it fell to the plate. "Oops! I'm so clumsy."

Hopefully she came across as the helpless flower he wanted her to be.

He raced around the table. "Are you okay?" Before she could answer, he grabbed her napkin and wiped her face and all down her front. "I think I got it all off."

It took her a moment to find her voice. "Sorry. I didn't mean to ruin the dress."

Mason looked her over. "You didn't. It all came off. Sure you're okay?"

She nodded. "Just embarrassed." But actually surprised. He was falling for her ruse.

He returned to his seat, breathing heavily. Then he ate a bite of the noodles.

It was safe.

She scarfed down the ones on her plate, not realizing just how famished she actually was until the food was in her mouth. At least she wouldn't have to make her escape on an empty stomach.

Mason watched her with interest as she ate. He took in his food slowly, but he did keep eating.

After she finished two platefuls—she hadn't meant to eat *that* much—she slumped in the chair, allowing her stomach to settle and readjust to not being hungry.

He set down his fork. "How are you feeling?"

"Better."

"Good." He gave her a Cheshire Cat grin. "Let me finish mine, then I'll get dessert."

"Sounds wonderful." She sat up straight and fluttered her lashes, getting back into her part.

Every time Mason looked down at his plate, Ava looked around. She couldn't see her belongings or an easy way out. Her only chance of escape appeared to be the front door or the windows by the bed, which were next to the door.

Thud!

Something hit the wall behind him.

She turned to Mason. "What was that?"

He wiped his mouth with a napkin. "Probably just a wild animal. What else could it be when we're in a cabin the middle of the woods?"

"You don't think someone could be trying to break in?"

"Not at all." He sipped his champagne and nodded toward hers. "Have some. It'll help you relax. There aren't any robbers. Nothing at all to worry about."

Other than the fact that he'd drugged her to get her here. And that she couldn't leave while he was watching with those hungry eyes.

Ava forced a smile and pretended to take a long sip. "You're right. This is nice."

Another thud sounded behind him, but neither acknowledged it. If someone broke in, it might be to her advantage. She could make her escape while Mason fought off the burglar.

He finally finished his food then got up and went to the fridge. While his back was turned, Ava swapped champagne glasses so that he got her full one. She again glanced around for anything helpful. Whatever he'd done with her things, they weren't in plain sight.

Mason brought over a chocolate cake. "I didn't make this. Hope you aren't too disappointed."

She shook her head. "I'm so full, I doubt I can eat much, anyway."

He frowned. "I was hoping we could feed it to each other."

Ava kept her disgust from showing on her face. "That sounds like fun." She rose and sat on his lap. "Let's do that."

His eyes widened. "You want to? I mean, okay."

She didn't wait for him to cut a piece. Instead, she grabbed his fork and took off a big piece.

Mason's eyes widened even more. "I'm not so sure—"

"Open up." She forced the dessert into his mouth, making sure to get it down his chin. Chocolate crumbled onto his white shirt. She covered her lips with two fingers. "Oops."

He glanced down. "Do you know much that cost?"

"I'm sorry." Ava kept her tone light. "I thought it'd be fun to feed you. Let me help." She wiped some cake from his face then grabbed his napkin and rubbed the chocolate creme into his dress shirt.

"What are you doing?" He jumped up, nearly knocking her over.

She stood and gave him the most innocent doe eyes she could muster. "I was trying to help. Don't be mad."

His expression softened. "No. I couldn't be upset with you."

Ava brought her hand to her heart. "Oh, good. Do you have another shirt? I feel so bad. Then we could start over. You feed me this time." She batted her lashes.

Mason smiled. "Let's do that." He held out his chair and gestured for her to sit, which she did. Then he hurried over to a cabinet and pulled a new shirt out of a travel bag. "I'll be right back."

"I'll be waiting."

He loosened his tie as he made his way to the bathroom, then closed the door behind him.

Ava leaped from the chair and bolted to the cabinet. Her bag rested next to his, but her shoes weren't there.

That would have to do.

She slid it over her shoulder then made her way to the door, taking just a moment to glance around for her shoes. Not seeing them, she quietly unlocked the door and flung it open.

What she saw made her stop in her tracks.

FLEE

Ava stared at the scene before her, too shocked to move. Her heart pounded like a jackhammer. They weren't in the middle of the woods. Not in a cabin.

A railing stood in front of her, showing a parking lot full of beat-up cars beyond it. Cigarette smoke, marijuana, and other smells hung in the air. Yelling sounded from not far away.

He'd brought her to a motel.

Thud!

No wild animals making noises against a cabin. Nobody trying to break in.

It was only neighbors. And any one of them could help her.

But she had to get away first. Hardly breathing, Ava tiptoed outside then closed the door behind her as quietly as she could. Three-fifty-one. The five was upside down.

She crept away and burst into a run once she was sure Mason wouldn't be able to hear her footsteps. Her lungs burned. Feet stung.

Ava kept her gaze low, making sure she didn't step on any needles lying around. She glanced behind her every so often to check that Mason wasn't following her. Once she reached stairs, she ran down, skipping every other one.

At the bottom, she dug through her bag, looking for her phone. The dead phone.

Her heart dropped. She tried to figure out what to do.

A police car raced down the street, sirens wailing.

The cops.

They would help her.

Ava ran toward the street. Waved her arms. But it was out of sight before she reached the sidewalk.

She glanced back at the hotel. Mason wasn't outside the room. Yet.

Goose bumps ran down her arms. She stepped over a pile of trash. Raced down the sidewalk. Tried to ignore her pained feet.

In an area like this, nobody would notice her screams. She couldn't let Mason catch up to her.

Cars zipped by. No more cop cars.

Sharp stones dug into her flesh. She winced. Pressed on.

A police cruiser! On the other side of the street.

Her pulse raced. She stopped. Waved furiously. Jumped up and down.

It drove right past her.

No...

Honk!

She whipped around.

The cop had turned around. Was now parked behind her, lights on but sirens off.

Tears stung. She blinked them back and ran to the car. Put her hand on the open passenger window. She didn't recognize the officer. That meant Mason had taken her to a different town. "Help! There's a man after me!"

The cop didn't even blink. "I don't see anyone."

"Please! I'm Captain Fleshman's daughter! It's on record that Mason Cooper has been stalking me."

"Captain Fleshman? Why does that sound familiar?"

"Nick Fleshman." She gave him other details.

His eyes lit up. "I know him! You're his daughter?"

"Yes! I swear, and Mason Cooper had me in that hotel back there. He drugged me to get me there after school."

"Do you have ID?"

Gasping for air, Ava dug through her purse and found her school identification card.

The officer glanced it over. "I'm going to need to call this in, Miss Fleshman." He got out and helped her into the back of the car.

She climbed onto the hard plastic seat, grateful to be where Mason couldn't reach her.

The cop called it in and got confirmation that she was telling the truth. Apparently her dad's force had everyone looking for her and Mason. He turned back to her. "Where did you say Mason Cooper took you?"

"That motel." She pointed to it. "Room three-fifty-one."

He called it in. Before he pulled away from the curb, two cruisers pulled into the lot with lights flashing. Then he turned to her. "I'm going to take you to your dad's station."

"Thank you."

The ride seemed to go on forever, even though the officer made light conversation. He was obviously trying to distract her, but she didn't care.

"Is Mason finally going to be locked up for good? I think this is his third arrest. Isn't it three strikes and you're out?"

"It isn't that simple, but if he's out on bail like you said, then he broke the terms. That means he won't be able to make bail again. He'll have to wait for his hearing behind bars."

Ava breathed a sigh of relief.

They made it to her dad's station, and everything was a blur of hugs as everyone from the receptionist to the officers all welcomed her back. Someone got her a blanket. Somebody else got her a first aid kit for her feet while a new officer took her statement.

"Where's my dad?"

She gave Ava a sympathetic smile. "On his way, sweetie. They were checking out a cabin where we thought you might've been taken."

The officer got Ava some snacks, and she ate mindlessly until her dad appeared in the doorway.

She leaped up. They both rushed across the room and into each other's arms.

Dad nearly squeezed the air out of her lungs. "How did he get to you?"

"He said someone was going to hurt Hanna if I didn't go with him. Then he drugged me to get me to that motel. He can't get out of jail again, can he?"

"No. He broke the terms of his bail."

"Can I go home now?"

"Yes, definitely. Let's go."

More people gave her hugs on the way out. Someone lent her a pair of shoes.

Dad held open the passenger door of his Mustang. "Where'd you get that dress?"

She groaned. "I don't want to talk about it."

"Okay, then. Let's just get you home. Want some takeout? Fettuccine Alfredo?"

"No. That's the last thing I want."

He gave her a funny look.

When they arrived home, Genevieve and Tinsley were there. Everyone hugged Ava, even Parker. Her heart warmed. No matter what genetics said about anyone, all of these people were her family.

TRAIL

Alex finished off the celebratory donut and took a deep breath. Everyone was settling back into the normal routine now that Ava was home safe and Mason was where he belonged, two towns over.

With everything quiet, he went back to the mommy blog. He'd told Sanchez everything he knew, and she was looking into it also. At least until they were called out again. They were checking missing persons databases for the blogger's kids.

She'd been smart, waiting to show pictures of the babies' faces. It made it harder to identify the missing kids since they changed so much in those early months.

He was about to walk around and stretch his legs when he froze. A missing baby picture came up close to Seattle that could've been the blogger's oldest.

Alex found the earliest photos of her, the girl called Willow, and compared them to the missing baby, Emily Amiya Wilkinson.

It could easily be the same baby.

He scooted his chair out toward Sanchez's desk. "Hey! Come look at this."

"You find something?" She hurried over. "What do you have?"

Alex showed her. "Same face, right?"

Her mouth gaped. "Has to be. Mackey! Come look at this."

Before long, all officers on duty agreed it was the same child. Everyone dug in, comparing pictures and studying the missing persons case.

Alex studied the sketch of the alleged kidnapper.

"Found another one!" Sanchez called out.

Alex nearly tripped over his feet, scrambling to her desk.

Sanchez compared images of the blogger's missing child as a baby to an infant reported missing near Spokane. "Everything fits. And again, looks like the same child."

Alex tugged on his hair. This was all the proof he needed. The other two kids obviously had to be abducted, as well. Even if not, the blogger was guilty of two counts of kidnapping. Not to mention whatever had happened to Connor, who was really Lucas Robert Adams.

The energy in the station grew to an excited buzz as everyone looked for the next missing child. Sanchez called the precincts where the missing kids had been abducted to report the findings.

Alex compared the two sketches of the kidnapper. The woman had the same features, though wildly different hair. Long straight black hair when she'd taken Connor and short curly blonde hair when she snatched Willow. She was also pale in one and tan in another.

Before long, they'd pinpointed each of the missing children. All taken from various locations in the state. Each time, the kidnapper wore a different disguise, but her facial features were the same. She was doing everything short of plastic surgery to change her appearance.

Alex studied the location of each abduction and drew lines from each one, connecting them to each other.

They all intersected in the middle of town.

STACY CLAFLIN

She was local.

The kids had to be close.

He jumped up. "They're in our jurisdiction!"

The other officers scrambled over, and Alex showed them what he had. Everyone spoke over each other. They all agreed she had to be near.

But where? That was the one thing they couldn't answer.

Alex leaned against the wall. "Do we give this information to the media? People will have to recognize her. She goes out all the time with these kids. It's going to be the quickest way to identify her."

Sanchez frowned. "Also the fastest way to send her running."

"She can only go so far if everyone is looking for her!" Alex leaned forward. "She's going to take another baby soon, if she hasn't already! We need to stop her now."

They debated, wasting time.

Alex reached for his phone. "I'm calling Nick. He'll know what to do."

"Don't bug him," Mackey said. "He just got his daughter back."

"He's the captain." Alex called Nick and filled him in on everything.

Nick agreed with Alex.

Alex ended the call. "He says to let the media know. We need the public's help on this."

It only took a few minutes for everyone to divide the responsibilities. At least they didn't have to contact the parents of the missing children—that was being handled locally. Alex's job was to post what they had on his blog. That would get the word out to people who were already looking for the woman.

He worked as quickly as he could, uploading the four police sketches of the woman along with current pictures of the kids from the latest blog posts. He shared the locations of the kidnappings along with the general area they suspected she was living currently. Then Alex urged the woman to give herself up. To return the children to the families where they belonged.

Alex read and re-read the post before publishing it. Despite the late hour, it started going viral right away. Pageviews, shares, and comments skyrocketed. Barely ten minutes later, it hit the news stations.

Now it was only a matter of waiting.

STRANGE

J ess kissed the kids. She turned to Willow. "Are you going to be okay watching them?"

She looked up from her book. "Always am."

"I shouldn't be long. This doctor's appointment is just a checkup after yesterday. If we're lucky, your new baby brother or sister will be out." She rubbed her oversized fake belly.

"Yay!" Daisy clapped. "I hope it's another girl."

"We'll see."

"When's Connor coming back?" Willow frowned.

Jess took a deep breath. "We talked about that."

"We miss him!"

"So do I, but that isn't going to bring him back from your mean daddy. That's what he is—mean. He takes one of you away. Daddies are awful, horrible people."

Willow's mouth formed a straight line.

Jess glanced at the time. "I'm running late. We'll discuss this later."

"Fine." Willow turned back to her book.

Annoyance stabbed at Jess. No sense in arguing with a kid. She'd probably forget about Connor once she saw the new baby, anyway. Willow was just being difficult because of the stress of the impending new family member. The kids often got edgy around this time of the pregnancy.

Without another word, Jess stormed out of the house. She needed to calm down, and quickly. The drive wasn't as far as usual. She was going to take a baby closer than normal.

This time, Jess was pretending to be a lactation consultant. She was going to try to interview a couple moms in a courtyard that was usually empty in the mornings.

Gravel flew from under the tires as she sped away. If she didn't hurry, she'd be late. She needed to arrive on time and appear calm and collected. Why did Willow have to give her lip on this morning, of all times?

No bother. She'd get herself in a good mood. Jess found her favorite playlist and sang along with her most loved songs. Then she imagined coming home with a new baby in tow. Finally taking off the fake belly. She really hated that thing. It made her back ache like crazy.

Halfway there, the gas light came on.

Jess swore. Why hadn't she checked that before she'd left?

No time to worry about that now. She pulled off the freeway and into the nearest gas station, adjusting her red wig and floppy hat before climbing out and filling up.

A couple at the next pump were whispering. Glancing over at her.

She glared at them. What was wrong with them? Was it because she wore a beach hat on an overcast day?

Once the tank was full, she flung the hat in the backseat and grabbed a baseball cap. Maybe that would be enough to get the attention off her. It was too bad she didn't use credit cards—too easy to be tracked—because she'd have loved nothing more than to be able to leave right then.

She headed inside to pay with cash. More patrons stared at her. Whispered. A kid pointed.

Had the world gone mad?

Jess tried to ignore them as she waited in line. She adjusted her sunglasses when she reached the cashier. "Pump eight."

"You new around here?"

"Just passing through." She handed him a fifty.

"Pump eight?"

"Yes! Just give me my change."

He didn't budge. More whispers sounded behind her.

"Never mind. Keep it." She stormed outside and peeled out of the parking lot. What was wrong with those people? Some kind of small town bias against outsiders? She'd have to remember to stay away unless her car was running on fumes.

Jess turned up the music and glanced at the GPS. Not too much farther. She needed to shake off her irritation before meeting with the first mom. This was no time for distractions or annoyances.

By the time she reached her destination, her mood had lifted for the most part. It was hard to shake it entirely. The whole morning had been off, first with the kids then at the gas station.

All she wanted was a baby! Was that really so much to ask? Did *everything* have to go against her? Hopefully these weren't signs that she shouldn't bother, that today wasn't her day. Didn't matter because she didn't believe in that superstitious crap.

The day would be what she made it. And today, she *would* come home with a baby. One way or another, she'd make sure of it.

In the parking lot, she checked all the pieces of her disguise. Everything looked good. She smiled in the mirror. It was strained thanks to the stress of the morning. No matter. She'd just have to push through it.

Going home empty-handed wasn't an option. Not today.

She hurried through the grass field to the courtyard. Empty as expected.

Nervous energy jolted through her. She walked around,

looking at flower arrangements and finally the fountain in the middle. Two sparrows bathed in it and played together. Their lighthearted banter help set her at ease.

Jess took a deep breath and focused on the sunlight warming her skin. The clouds had broken and everything was brighter. That was a sign she'd be happy to take if she was into superstition. But she made her own destiny. Life had tried to prevent her from having a family, but she'd shown life. Today she would get her *fifth* child.

Sure, Connor was no longer with them but he was still her second child. She would always mourn his loss. And she would hold onto the fact that she was the only one with the treasured knowledge of what had really happened. Only she knew. Nobody else. Just her.

Footsteps sounded from behind.

Jess's heart raced. She took a deep breath and focused on the image of placing a sweet baby in the car seat in the back of her car.

She turned around and smiled. "Are you Shay?"

The young mom pushing the jogging stroller stopped and smiled. "I am. You're Jess?"

Jess held out her hand and nodded. "It's a pleasure to meet you. Do you want to sit over there?" She gestured toward some tables and chairs.

Shay's brows drew together as she studied Jess. Her smile melted. "You're a lactation consultant?"

Jess's heart rate sped up. "Yes. If we're a good fit, I can come to your home and help you with your breastfeeding."

"You have references?"

"Plenty. Did you see my website?"

Shay didn't respond. She pulled some hair behind her ear. Swallowed. Her face lost some color. "Um, you know what? I think I'm going to keep trying on my own for a while instead. I'll give you a call if I still need help later."

She spun around and ran the other way.

Jess's heart sank. Where had she gone wrong? Maybe she needed to go back to snatching random babies. Or perhaps she needed to stick with her plan.

One way or another, she would get her baby.

CLOSE

Alex pressed the phone between his shoulder and ear. "Thank you for calling. Do you have anything else to tell us about the woman you saw at the gas station?"

"No. But she looks exactly like those sketches on the news."

"I appreciate you calling. And we can reach out to you if we have more questions?"

"Of course. I hope you catch her!"

Alex repeated the phone number. "Is that a good number to reach you at?"

"Yeah."

He thanked her again and ended the call.

"Sure you won't go home?" Nick handed him a steaming foam cup.

Alex sipped the coffee. "Not a chance. I've been on the blogger's trail too long. We know she was at that gas station this morning. She's this close!" Alex held his finger and thumb a hair width apart.

Nick nodded. "If you need a nap, feel free to crash on my couch. Can't guarantee my office will be quiet, but it's a comfy couch."

"I'm not sleeping until she's behind bars and the kids are returned to their parents."

"That last part could be a while." Nick leaned against Alex's desk. "Social services will have to get involved. You know how it goes."

"Yeah. Fine, I'll sleep once the kids are safe. How's that?"

"Sounds good. I—"

"We know where she is!" Chang shouted. "A woman just spoke with her in a courtyard an hour away! She thinks she was going to try to take her infant. Our suspect was posing as a lactation consultant. I've just alerted that precinct."

The entire office went into a frenzy of activity after Chang finished giving all the details from the call he'd just taken.

Alex's heart raced. They were so close to catching her! A sense of pride swelled in him. If he hadn't insisted following the tips, the blogger would be taking another baby that very day. Actually, she still could.

Anything was possible until she was captured.

Alex turned to his laptop and updated his blog. He'd never posted four times in one day about the same case before, but a lot of people were refreshing his page for the latest updates. Even the news sources were getting their information from it.

Crazy times he was living in. Alex never would've dreamed any of this was possible just a few years earlier.

He quickly reviewed the latest, urging people in the area to look for her in any of her disguises. She could have red, brown, blonde, or black hair. Or even something different altogether. He wouldn't have been surprised if she shaved her head at this point.

New comments flooded his updated post. Alex could hardly keep up as he sorted through them, trying to find any that had new information. Despite him encouraging his readers to call his precinct with tips, some insisted on leaving them in his comments.

He finished off his coffee and walked around, listening to the chatter of people on the phone, taking calls about the case. Despite his racing heart, his eyelids were growing heavy.

Maybe a power nap was what he needed. He slid into the captain's office.

Nick, on the phone, nodded toward the couch.

Alex sprawled out and pulled a dark blue crocheted blanket over himself, closing his eyes. Sleep overtook him right away.

Conversation woke him. He glanced at the clock.

Two hours! He'd slept that long?

Alex bolted upright. "What's going on?"

"We have a location." Chang glanced at his phone.

Nick rose from his chair. "She's still posing as a lactation consultant, but now she's at someone's home. And the mom is trying to hold her until officers arrive."

Alex jumped to his feet. "Where is she?"

Chang's expression tightened. "Here in town."

"What?" Alex's stomach knotted. "She's actually here?"

"Let's go!"

"That's what we're doing!"

Everyone raced for the cruisers. Alex went with Nick, and they led the way, sirens blaring. Once they neared the neighborhood, everyone silenced them but left the lights on. They pulled up to the house, blocking the driveway and the cars in it.

Alex's heart raced. They were about to catch a kidnapper that had started out as a clue given to him through his blog.

They got out of the cars and crept around the house. He and Nick headed for the front door. Alex looked inside the window. Just as he did, the door opened.

A woman with a baby in a wrap carrier stepped out. "She just left. I don't know if she got spooked because I was trying to keep her here, or if she figured out what I was doing, but she's gone. I'm sorry."

"You did great," Nick said. "Did you happen to see what kind of car she was driving?"

"Her car's still in my driveway. She ran out my back door!"

Nick and Alex exchanged a quick glance.

"Which way did she go?" Nick demanded.

The woman led them through her house to the backyard and pointed toward the woods.

Always with the woods.

They burst into a run, both scaling the fence then drawing their weapons. Alex called in the update and the other officers on the scene headed for the woods.

Nick nudged Alex and pointed to fresh footprints.

They both burst into a run, following them.

RACE

J ess pressed a palm against a tree and gasped for air. Her legs burned. Back ached. She needed to lose the fake belly. It was weighing her down. Making everything harder. She could barely breathe.

It would be tough explaining to the kids why she wasn't pregnant anymore, yet didn't have a baby, either. But that would be better than getting caught and going to jail. Then who would take care of her children?

She needed her new baby. This was just a kink in her plans.

Jess lifted her shirt and removed the belly. She set it behind a bush so she could come back for it later. Once she'd gotten away and nobody was after her.

Now she'd be able to run. Her whole body felt better. Free.

Leaves rustled not far away.

She bolted in the opposite direction. It felt like she was moving at twice the speed as before. Like she could run and never have to stop.

"Stop!"

Her heart skipped a beat.

The last thing she was going to do was to give up. She would get away and hide until the cops left and she could get back to her car and go home. Or she could just walk. It wasn't that far. But first she had to lose them.

Jess glanced back. Two uniformed men were behind her. Yelling at her.

She darted behind every tree and bush she could find. Nothing would keep her from getting back home to her kids. Not the cops, not anything.

"We've got you surrounded!"

Liars. No way they could be on every side. They were in the middle of the woods.

Jess ducked behind a bush and stayed put, breathing hard. She did her best to stay quiet, though her lungs cried out. Her throat was parched.

The cops ran right past.

She breathed a sigh of relief and out of habit put her hands where her belly should've been protruding. Instead, her palms landed on her shirt. She muttered curses at the police.

Why couldn't they just leave well enough alone? Couldn't those jackals pick on someone other than a pregnant single mom? Jerks. The whole lot of them.

After her breathing returned to normal, she listened.

Everything was quiet.

All the cops must've run on past.

Jess couldn't go in the same direction. Either she'd catch up with them or they'd double back and find her. She also couldn't go back to the house for her car. No doubt they'd either blocked it in —she never should've parked in the driveway—or one of them was waiting for her.

Why couldn't they find a real criminal to go after? All she was doing was trying to raise a family. None of them had any idea how hard it was to be a single mom.

She was left with only one choice. Going through the woods a different route. Hoping she came out close to home or somewhere familiar. If she was lucky, these woods might even connect to the ones she lived in. They were near enough. It was possible. Unlikely, but possible.

Regardless, she needed to do something. Sitting in the same spot only heightened her chances of being found.

She rose and stepped out from behind the bush.

The barrels of two guns faced her.

Two cops aimed their weapons at her. The younger one looked familiar. It took a moment to place him. She'd seen his face on a blog.

Alexander.

"Hands in the air!"

Jess didn't budge.

"Raise your hands!"

She spun around and ran.

Bang!

A bullet whizzed past her so fast she felt its wind. It was so loud, it made her ears ring.

Her bladder emptied. Urine ran down her legs, soaking into her pants.

"Stop! Next one won't miss. That was your only warning shot!"

Jess skidded to a stop and turned around slowly.

"Hands in the air!" Alexander's brows drew together. "Now!"

She swallowed and put her palms up. Then she glanced down at her pants. "Look. My water just broke! You need to get me to the hospital."

"You don't look pregnant. Get your hands up higher!"

"I'm just a single mom trying to raise my kids. Let me be!"

The cops stepped closer with their guns still aimed at her.

She screamed at the top of her lungs. Louder, and louder still, until her throat was raw.

Alexander cuffed her while the other guy took her purse and held her down.

"Don't touch me like that! Perverts!"

"Shut up," one of them said. She couldn't tell who.

They dragged her toward the house. She continued yelling accusations. No way was she going down without a fight.

Alexander shoved her into the back of the police car while the other guy read her rights.

Rights. That was a joke. If she had any rights, she'd be free to go home.

"Where are the kids?" Alexander demanded from the front passenger seat.

"I'll never tell you." She folded her arms. "You'll never get my kids."

He scoffed. "*Your* kids?"

She narrowed her eyes. "Yes, *mine.*"

The other guy turned around. "Who's going to take care of them when you're in jail?"

"Not your concern." Jess looked out the window.

"You want them to die?" Alexander yelled. "We know from your blog that you live alone with them."

"Willow's perfectly capable of taking care of them."

"What about when they run out of food?"

Jess turned to him as a brilliant idea struck her. Why hadn't she thought of this before? "Let me go, and I'll tell you."

"You're never getting out of jail after what you've done. And if we find out that you've killed Connor, you might just get worse than a life sentence."

"I didn't kill him!"

"But he *is* dead?"

She looked away.

"Now you're going to take your right to be silent?"

She didn't respond.

"Where are the kids?"

"I want immunity."

"Nope."

Jess glared at him. "I'm going to sue you personally. Take everything you value."

"Really? How?"

"Because you're harassing a single mom! How will that sound in the papers?"

Alexander turned to the other guy. "I think she's delusional."

"You *think*?"

They both laughed, then Alexander held up her purse. "Your purse is vibrating. Think the kids you abducted are trying to reach you?"

"There's no phone there, Einstein. Think I'm dumb enough to leave something there that could be tracked?"

"Let's see."

The other officer turned a sharp corner, and she hit her head on the hard plastic seat.

Alexander pulled out her phone and stared at the screen, his face paling.

Jess's mind raced, trying to figure out what could scare him like that. "What?"

He stared her down. "This alert says there's a fire at your house!"

Her throat closed up. Then she realized he was playing her. "Liar!"

Alexander shoved the phone up to the bars separating them.

He was telling the truth. The alarm system app showed a fire.

Her kids were actually in danger.

"Am I ever getting out of jail?"

They both shook their heads no.

The kids were better off staying where they were in that case. If she couldn't have them, nobody could. Nobody could love them or care for them like she could. "I'm not telling you anything."

Jess sucked in her lips, determined to use her right to remain silent.

FIRE

Nick radioed in what little they knew about the fire. He told them the name of the app, in hopes that they could use that to find the address.

Alex notified the local fire departments, but none of them knew of any fires. He turned to the back seat. "Are you playing us? Is the app a fake, to throw us off?"

In the rear-view mirror, Nick saw the woman suck in her lips and close her eyes.

"Don't you care about the children's well-being?" Nick squeezed the steering wheel. "*Your* children, as you said. They're in a burning building!"

She hummed.

Nick counted silently and glanced over at Alex, who looked as furious as he felt.

Alex turned more toward the kidnapper. "You know what? I have three kids, and if any of them was in danger, I'd do whatever it took to keep them safe! I've even risked my own life! How can you do this?"

She hummed louder.

Nick took a deep breath. "Because she knows she isn't *really* their mom."

"Shut up! I'm their only parent—the only person who cares about them."

"Not true!" Alex growled. "Right now, we care about them more than you do. We're trying to save them."

New information came in over the radio. They had a location for the house, and Nick and Alex were the closest ones to it.

Nick made a sharp right turn. "Change of plans."

After a few more turns, they came to a dirt path. Pines and maples on both sides shadowed the long driveway.

Smoke rose from above the trees in front of them.

Nick held his breath and hit the gas, spraying dirt behind the car.

Alex radioed in that they had a visual.

The large two-story home looked like a log cabin. The dark smoke came from the back of the house. There were no flames visible from the front.

Nick slammed on the breaks, and both he and Alex flung open their doors.

"What about me?"

Alex turned to her. "You get to watch. And if they don't make it, you get to live with it being your fault!"

"Not if I—"

Nick slammed his door, not wanting to hear another word from her. He glanced at Alex. "See if you can get in the front. I'm going to look around back."

"Be careful!" Alex ran up the steps.

Nick raced around the building, looking for both flames and a way inside. There were no windows on this side of the house. But around back there were windows galore. He just needed to find something to break one with if the kids were unable to let him in.

He pounded on the sliding glass door and looked inside. No kids were in sight. "Police! We're here to help!"

Smoke was filling the air, but there were still no visible flames. Nick pounded some more, calling out the same thing.

Nothing.

Boom!

Glass shattered to his right. The pieces fell down from the second level. Flames burst out from the broken windows.

His heart jumped into his throat. There were up to four kids inside, maybe more if she'd abducted more than they knew about. He looked around for something to break the glass.

There was a pile of firewood leaning about the house.

Nick ran over and grabbed a piece. He shoved it against a window, knowing that would be easier to break than the door. The window cracked, but didn't shatter.

He took a deep breath and threw all his strength into the task. The wood went straight through with such force he let go and it flew against a wall inside.

Sirens wailed in the distance.

"Hurry!" Nick knocked the rest of the broken shards free of the frame with another piece of firewood, then, careful not to slice himself, climbed in. The smoke made his eyes water. He covered his mouth and nose with his arm and raced from room to room, calling out to the children, making sure not to breathe in the smoke.

He came to the front door, unlocking and opening it for Alex. Sirens sounded louder outside.

"Did you find them?"

Nick shook his head and pointed to the stairs. "Check up there!"

Alex covered his face and ran up.

Nick turned back around to search the rest of the downstairs. "Is anyone down here? I'm here to help!"

He checked closets, behind couches, and everywhere he could think that a scared child might hide.

Crash!

That was upstairs.

Nick spun around.

A whimper sounded behind him.

He froze. Spun back around.

Another whimper.

"Is someone down here?"

Nothing.

Nick crept toward where he'd heard the noises. Two little bare feet stuck out from underneath a curtain.

His heart skipped a beat. He leaped over and pulled aside the curtain.

A little girl, no more than two or three, huddled with a teddy bear. Her eyes widened.

Nick squatted and reached for her. "I'm a policeman, sweetie. I need to get you out of here."

She cowered, clung to the toy.

"I'm a daddy. Let me help you."

The girl scooted away, shaking her head. "Daddies are bad people."

Nick hesitated. What had that woman taught the kids? "No. Daddies love and help kids. Let me help you."

She moved farther away, squeezing the bear harder.

Another crash sounded upstairs.

Nick scooped her up, and headed for the door. "Is there anyone else down here with you?"

The girl kicked and screamed.

He ran outside, choking in the fresh air.

A fire engine pulled up and an aid car followed behind.

The little girl continued struggling against Nick. "Mommy!" She reached for the car where her kidnapper smirked at Nick.

He handed the child off to a paramedic and told one of the firefighters what he knew of the situation inside. Two or three more kids and an officer. He didn't know where the fire was, other than upstairs.

Two more fire units arrived. Firefighters flooded into the house.

Alex ran outside with a girl in one arm and a toddler in the other. He gave them to the medics and struggled to breathe.

"You okay?" Nick guided him to the ambulance and instructed someone to check him out for smoke inhalation. Then he marched back over to the cruiser and faced the kidnapper. "We rescued three kids. Are there any more?"

She looked away.

"Are there any more?" Nick shouted. "You took at least four kids! People have accused you of killing one. Are there more children in the house?"

She glared at him. "I didn't kill Connor!"

"Is he alive?"

Her mouth formed a straight line. "No. It's just those three. I want a lawyer."

"You're going to need one." He slammed the door and called in the information, then told the head firefighter on the scene.

Alex came over. "Are all the kids out?"

"If she's telling the truth." He glared at their suspect.

"What'd she say?" Alex's expression tightened.

"She says one of the kids is dead."

"Connor?"

Nick nodded.

"How?"

"All she said was that she didn't kill him. She's not saying another word until she has an attorney."

"Of course not." Alex jutted his jaw. "You got Daisy out?"

"Little girl, about three."

"Good." He glared at the blogger. "At least we know she's never getting out after everything she's done."

"Let's hope her attorney isn't that good."

"Speaking of. Let's get her to the station and book her."

"Nothing would make me happier."

"What about some shut-eye?" Nick arched a brow.

Alex nodded. "After all this, I could sleep for a week."

"Take tomorrow off, my friend."

DECISION

Alex tapped his glass against Nick's. They'd just received word that all three kids had been returned to their families. As glad as he was for the kids and their families, there was one family devastated. They had closure, a body to bury properly, but no child to embrace.

That was where Connor—Lucas—should've gone. His parents' arms. Not the county morgue. Not a cemetery. His heart ached for those parents.

He glanced over at Ariana building a sandcastle for Laney and Zander. She played peekaboo with them as she built, and they both burst into fits of laughter each time, nearly falling onto the blanket they sat on underneath the huge colorful umbrella.

Nick glanced at his phone. "Shouldn't Zoey and Genevieve be back by now?"

Alex sipped his cherry soda. "I'd be surprised if they don't end up meeting us at the restaurant. They're looking at wedding dresses, remember?"

Nick grinned. "That's true. Genevieve's really enjoying the whole planning process." He glanced at the time again. "We should have the kids reapply sunscreen."

They called everyone over and lathered everyone up again. Ari smeared the lotion on the babies while Alex got her back. Hanna and Tinsley helped each other out while Parker insisted on doing his himself. Ava and Braylon slathered one another, laughing.

"Wait before going into the water!" Nick called as the kids scattered.

Alex opened a new pop. "Ava seems to be doing well after her ordeal."

Nick nodded. "She insists she wasn't abducted. Says it was nothing like before. She's upset with me for making her go back to counseling."

"She'll thank you later."

"That's what I keep telling myself."

They sat in silence watching the kids for a few moments before Nick turned to Alex and took a deep breath. His expression was serious, pensive.

"Uh, oh." Alex dug his pop bottle into the sand. "What's up?"

Nick drew in a deep breath and glanced over at Parker. "I decided to do the paternity test. I haven't been able to stop thinking about it since we went to the prison and spoke with Dave. I need to know for myself. And Parker deserves the truth, either way. If he has a completely different set of genetics, it's his right to know." Nick played with a loose string on his shirt. "If mental illness runs in his gene pool, he should know that, too. And if there's anything in Dave's medical history, we need that information. It's only fair to him."

Alex nodded. Unfortunately, he knew all that too well. He glanced over at Zander, who carried Dave's genetics.

"It won't change anything," Nick said. "Parker's still my son, regardless. Doesn't matter who supplied half his DNA. He's mine. I'd give my life for him in a heartbeat."

"You're preaching to the choir."

"So, you think I'm making the right choice?"

"Yeah. It's the hard one, but the right one."

"Good. Because I already had it done."

Alex gave him a double-take. "When do you find out?"

Nick looked over at Parker. "I already have the results. I haven't looked at them yet. The question is, do I check before telling him? Or do I tell him, then we check together?"

"That's a tough one. If he's yours—you know, genetically—then there's no point in even bringing it up. He doesn't need to know that it was ever a question."

"Corrine could still tell him one day."

"Then you'd be able to show him proof that he's yours."

Nick scrunched his face. "I suppose."

"If you want us to watch the other kids while you talk to Parker, we will. Just say the word. It's going to be a big conversation."

"That it will. I'll let you know if I need to take you up on the offer."

"Hopefully you won't." Alex looked at Zander, dreading the day he would have to have a similar conversation.

YOU MAY ENJOY...

If you're enjoying the Alex Mercer series, you'll probably also really like my standalone novel, *Lies Never Sleep*.

Two friends enter an abandoned insane asylum hoping to make a viral video... Instead, they disappear. As friends and family search for them, unexpected secrets come to light. Some secrets are darker than others, but everyone is a suspect. When the truth finally comes out, will the boys be found dead or alive?

Excerpt

Atlas James hesitated at the edge of the property as they crept through the rusty wrought-iron gate. His heart thundered in his chest, both from nerves and excitement. The phone shook in his hand as he captured the video.

Emmett Powell turned around, wide-eyed and grinning, though it was barely visible in the moonlight. "You ready?"

Atlas didn't want to admit his nerves were getting the best of him. "It's gonna be awesome."

"Right? And best of all, we'll finally be famous. This video is going to go viral for sure. We'd better get going before midnight strikes." Emmett pushed aside some old vines growing up and protruding from the trees, then opened the second gate—the owners of the insane asylum had been serious about keeping the residents locked inside. It creaked in protest.

"Try to keep up." Atlas rushed past Emmett down the uneven path. It had probably once been a perfectly-level walkway, but roots and decades had changed that.

Emmett caught up to him. "You think anyone else is here? I mean, it *is* the anniversary of the slayings."

As far as Atlas knew, nobody else had ever been brave—or stupid—enough to break into the old building on this date. "I think we're good."

"If we don't get killed, right?" Emmett laughed and whacked Atlas on the back.

"Right." Atlas aimed his phone at the old asylum.

The large abandoned building loomed before them, partially blocking their view of the moon. It looked more like a mansion than a mental hospital, but rumor had it, that was how it had started... until the original owner went crazy and killed his family and servants. Then his house became a mental hospital after no potential homeowners would buy it.

Emmett held up his phone and aimed it at himself. "Atlas and I are here on the anniversary of the Ichabod slayings. We're the first to attempt this, and we're going to try to lure out old Dr. Ichabod himself. Or maybe even the original owner of the building. What you're about to see is history!"

Atlas glanced over at the building. After having only walked a little way, the moon was now directly over the building.

Emmett continued speaking into the phone as they made their way closer to the towering building. It was even taller and creepier up close.

They both skidded to a stop as they reached the steps leading to the front door. Emmett turned his phone toward the building, giving more narrative before pausing the recording.

Atlas held his breath, trying to calm his pounding heart. If this kept up, it would burst through his chest. The sound echoed in his ears, drowning out everything in the night. Even Emmett's voice. He turned toward his friend. "What?"

"You ready?"

He studied the building, and a chill ran down his back. Rumors and stories he'd heard since childhood spun through his mind. As much as he wanted a viral video, he hoped they wouldn't actually run into any murderous spirits. Ghosts didn't exist, right? With any luck, they'd just find some cool relics and the video would still make them famous. "Yeah, of course. Can't wait to see what's in there."

Emmett marched up the steps like he owned the place.

Atlas swallowed and pulled some of his hair behind his ears.

It was the moment of truth. Everything in him screamed to run away. But he was no chicken. Not only that, they'd planned this for months. He couldn't let Emmett down. Besides, they might actually go viral. And if they didn't do this now, they'd have to wait another year for the anniversary of the sanitarium's closing.

Another year for the anniversary of the massacre at Ichabod Insane Asylum.

Atlas caught up with Emmett. Each step felt like it would break under their weight. None did.

"What are we going to do if it's locked?" Atlas stared at the enormous door with several deadbolts.

"It's not." Emmett spoke with the confidence of experience.

"How do you know? Have you already been here? Did you come here without me?"

"The locks were all broken when that doctor killed everyone, remember? People tried to escape, but nobody made it off the property that day alive. The police broke all the locks to get inside. The sight was so terrifying, several of them passed out."

Atlas shuddered. What would they find? Old blood stains? Murder weapons?

"Ninety years ago tonight." A thread of excitement ran through Emmett's voice. "And we're here!"

Atlas questioned his sanity, but pushed the thoughts aside. It was just an abandoned building. Ghosts weren't real. The anniversary was no more significant than any other day.

He hoped.

Emmett reached for the doorknob.

More information: https://stacyclaflin.com/books/lies-never-sleep/

OTHER BOOKS BY STACY CLAFLIN

You may enjoy some of Stacy Claflin's other books, also. She's a *USA Today* bestselling author who writes about complex characters overcoming incredible odds. Whether it's her Gone saga of psychological thrillers, her various paranormal romance tales, or her romances, Stacy's three-dimensional characters shine through bringing an experience readers don't soon forget.

The Gone Saga
The Gone Trilogy: Gone, Held, Over

Dean's List

No Return

Alex Mercer Thrillers
Girl in Trouble

Turn Back Time

Little Lies

Against All Odds

Don't Forget Me

Tainted Love

Curse of the Moon
Lost Wolf

Chosen Wolf

Hunted Wolf

Broken Wolf

Cursed Wolf

Secret Jaguar

Valhalla's Curse

Renegade Valkyrie

Pursued Valkyrie

Silenced Valkyrie

Vengeful Valkyrie

Unleashed Valkyrie

The Transformed Series

Main Series

Deception

Betrayal

Forgotten

Ascension

Duplicity

Sacrifice

Destroyed

Transcend

Entangled

Dauntless

Obscured

Partition

Standalones

Fallen

Silent Bite

Hidden Intentions

Saved by a Vampire

Sweet Desire

Short Story Collection

Tiny Bites

The Hunters
Seaside Surprises

Seaside Heartbeats

Seaside Dances

Seaside Kisses

Seaside Christmas

Bayside Wishes

Bayside Evenings

Bayside Promises

Bayside Destinies

Bayside Opposites

Bayside Mistletoe

Indigo Bay
Sweet Dreams

Sweet Reunion

Sweet Complications

Standalones
Lies Never Sleep

Dex

Haunted

Fall into Romance

AUTHOR'S NOTE

Thanks so much for reading *Tainted Love*. I know it's been a little bit of a wait since the last book. (Unless you're new to the series, then you didn't have to wait!) I'm excited to be back in this story world and am looking forward to writing more Alex Mercer novels this year than I did last year. So, keep your eyes open for a new one soon!

I'd love to hear from you. The easiest way to do that is to join my mailing list (link below) and reply to any of the emails.

If you enjoyed this book, please consider leaving a review wherever you purchased it. Not only will your review help me to better understand what you like—so I can give you more of it!—but it will also help other readers find my work. Reviews can be short— just share your honest thoughts. That's it.

Want to know when I have a new release? Sign up here for new release updates. You'll also get a free book! http://stacyclaflin.com/newsletter/

Thank you for your support! I really appreciate it—and you guys!

ABOUT THE AUTHOR

Stacy Claflin is a USA Today bestselling author who writes about complex women overcoming incredible odds. Whether it's her Gone saga of psychological thrillers, her various paranormal romance tales, or her sweet romance series, Stacy's three-dimensional characters shine through.

Decades after she wrote her first stories on construction paper and years after typing on an inherited green screen computer that weighed half a ton, Stacy realized her dream of becoming a full-time bestselling author.

When she's not busy writing or educating her kids from home, Stacy enjoys watching a wide variety of shows like Reign, Supernatural, Walking Dead, The Originals, Designated Survivor, Pretty Little Liars, Stranger Things, Haven, and Once Upon a Time.

For more information:
stacyclaflin.com/about

Made in the USA
Columbia, SC
28 July 2019